Breath, Eyes, Memory

ʌʌʌʌʌʌʌʌ

Edwidge Danticat

An *Abacus* Book

First published in the United States of America by Soho Press 1994
First published in Great Britain by Abacus 1995
This edition published by Abacus 1996

A CIP catalogue record for this book is available
from the British Library.

ISBN 0 349 10682 7

Printed and bound in Great Britain by Clays Ltd, St Ives plc.

Abacus
A Division of
Little, Brown and Company (UK)
Brettenham House
Lancaster Place
London WC2E 7EN

..., many of them ....scape
...... Haiti as their subject. Her award-winning short
...... now appeared in over twenty-five periodicals, and she
..... the holder of a James Michener Fellowship. *Breath Eyes,
Memory* is her first novel. Her new collection of stories, *Krik?
Krak!* was nominated for the 1995 National Book Award.

A graduate of Barnard College and the Brown University Writing
Program, Edwidge Danticat now lives in Brooklyn, New York.

Praise for *Breath, Eyes, Memory*

'Danticat's calm clarity of vision takes on the resonance of folk art.
In the end, her book achieves an emotional complexity that lifts
it out of the realm of the potboiler and into that of poetry. The
tale is lovingly dominated by powerful female characters who
struggle to make better lives for themselves and their families ...
extraordinarily successful.'

New York Times Book Review

'A novel that rewards the reader again and again with small but
exquisite and unforgettable epiphanies ... This quiet soul-penetrating
story about four generations of women trying to hold on to one
another in the Haitian diaspora ... is loaded with folk wisdom and
fairy tales, the imagery of fear and pain, and an understated political subtext that makes this first novel much, much more than the
elementary domestic story it might have been.'

Washington Post

Also by Edwidge Danticat

KRIK? KRAK!

To the brave women of Haiti,
grandmothers, mothers, aunts,
sisters, cousins, daughters, and friends,
on this shore and other shores.
We have stumbled but we will not fall.

Much thanks to my father and mother, André and Rose Danticat. My brothers Kelly, Karl, and Eliab André. My cousins Nick and Jean. My uncle Joseph and Aunt Denise in Haiti. My uncle Franck here. My uncle Max, wherever you are.

Much thanks to the old gang, Chantal, Maryse, Stephanie, Michele and Sandra. The whole gang at Barnard! Suzanne Guard—my guardian angel. To Christopher Dunn for muito amor and support. And Laura Hruska, for believing I could.

One

Chapter 1

∧∧∧∧∧∧∧∧∧

A flattened and drying daffodil was dangling off the little card that I had made my aunt Atie for Mother's Day. I pressed my palm over the flower and squashed it against the plain beige cardboard. When I turned the corner near the house, I saw her sitting in an old rocker in the yard, staring at a group of children crushing dried yellow leaves into the ground. The leaves had been left in the sun to dry. They would be burned that night at the konbit potluck dinner.

I put the card back in my pocket before I got to the yard. When Tante Atie saw me, she raised the piece of white cloth she was embroidering and waved it at me. When I stood in front of her, she opened her arms just wide enough for my body to fit into them.

"How was school?" she asked, with a big smile.

She bent down and kissed my forehead, then pulled me down onto her lap.

"School was all right," I said. "I like everything but those reading classes they let parents come to in the afternoon. Everybody's parents come except you. I never have anyone to read with, so Monsieur Augustin always pairs me off with an old lady who wants to learn her letters, but does not have children at the school."

"I do not want a pack of children teaching me how to read," she said. "The young should learn from the old. Not the other way. Besides, I have to rest my back when you have your class. I have work."

A blush of embarrassment rose to her brown cheeks.

"At one time, I would have given anything to be in school. But not at my age. My time is gone. Cooking and cleaning, looking after others, that's my school now. That schoolhouse is your school. Cutting cane was the only thing for a young one to do when I was your age. That is why I never want to hear you complain about your school." She adjusted a pink head rag wrapped tightly around her head and dashed off a quick smile revealing two missing side teeth. "As long as you do not have to work in the fields, it does not matter that I will never learn to read that ragged old Bible under my pillow."

Whenever she was sad, Tante Atie would talk about the sugar cane fields, where she and my mother practically lived when they were children. They saw people die there from sunstroke every day. Tante Atie said that, one day while they were all working together, her father—my grandfather—stopped to wipe his forehead, leaned forward, and died. My grandmother took the body in her arms and tried to scream the life back into it. They all kept screaming and hollering, as

4

my grandmother's tears bathed the corpse's face. Nothing would bring my grandfather back.

The bòlèt man was coming up the road. He was tall and yellow like an amber roach. The children across the road lined up by the fence to watch him, clutching one another as he whistled and strolled past them.

This albino, whose name was Chabin, was the biggest lottery agent in the village. He was thought to have certain gifts that had nothing to do with the lottery, but which Tante Atie believed put the spirits on his side. For example, if anyone was chasing him, he could turn into a snake with one flip of his tongue. Sometimes, he could see the future by looking into your eyes, unless you closed your soul to him by thinking of a religious song and prayer while in his presence.

I could tell that Tante Atie was thinking of one of her favorite verses as he approached. *Death is the shepherd of man and in the final dawn, good will be the master of evil.*

"*Honneur, mes belles,* Atie, Sophie."

Chabin winked at us from the front gate. He had no eyelashes—or seemed to have none. His eyebrows were tawny and fine like corn silk, but he had a thick head of dirty red hair.

"How are you today?" he asked.

"Today, we are fine," Tante Atie said. "We do not know about tomorrow."

"*Ki niméro* today?" he asked. "What numbers you playing?"

"Today, we play my sister Martine's age," Tante Atie said.

5

"Sophie's mother's age. Thirty-one. Perhaps it will bring me luck."

"Thirty-one will cost you fifty cents," he said.

Tante Atie reached into her bra and pulled out one *gourde*.

"We will play the number twice," she said.

Even though Tante Atie played faithfully, she had never won at the *bòlèt*. Not even a small amount, not even once.

She said the lottery was like love. Providence was not with her, but she was patient.

The albino wrote us a receipt with the numbers and the amount Tante Atie had given him.

The children cringed behind the gate as he went on his way. Tante Atie raised her receipt towards the sun to see it better.

"There, he wrote your name," I said pointing to the letters, "and there, he wrote the number thirty-one."

She ran her fingers over the numbers as though they were quilted on the paper.

"Would it not be wonderful to read?" I said for what must have been the hundredth time.

"I tell you, my time is passed. School is not for people my age."

The children across the street were piling up the leaves in Madame Augustin's yard. The bigger ones waited on line as the smaller ones dropped onto the pile, bouncing to their feet, shrieking and laughing. They called one another's names: Foi, Hope, Faith, Espérance, Beloved, God-Given, My Joy, First Born, Last Born, Aséfi, Enough-Girls, Enough-Boys, Deliverance, Small Misery, Big Misery, No Misery. Names as bright and colorful as the giant poincianas in Madame Augustin's garden.

They grabbed one another and fell to the ground, rejoicing as though they had flown past the towering flame trees that shielded the yard from the hot Haitian sun.

"You think these children would be kind to their mothers and clean up those leaves," Tante Atie said. "Instead, they are making a bigger mess."

"They should know better," I said, secretly wishing that I too could swim in their sea of dry leaves.

Tante Atie threw her arms around me and squeezed me so hard that the lemon-scented perfume, which she dabbed across her chest each morning, began to tickle my nose.

"Sunday is Mother's Day, *non?*" she said, loudly sucking her teeth. "The young ones, they should show their mothers they want to help them. What you see in your children today, it tells you about what they will do for you when you are close to the grave."

I appreciated Tante Atie, but maybe I did not show it enough. Maybe she wanted to be a real mother, have a real daughter to wear matching clothes with, hold hands and learn to read with.

"Mother's Day will make you sad, won't it, Tante Atie?"

"Why do you say that?" she asked.

"You look like someone who is going to be sad."

"You were always wise beyond your years, just like your mother."

She gently held my waist as I climbed down from her lap. Then she cupped her face in both palms, her elbows digging into the pleats of her pink skirt.

I was going to sneak the card under her pillow Saturday night so that she would find it as she was making the bed on

Sunday morning. But the way her face drooped into her palms made me want to give it to her right then.

I dug into my pocket, and handed it to her. Inside was a poem that I had written for her.

She took the card from my hand. The flower nearly fell off. She pressed the tape against the short stem, forced the baby daffodil back in its place, and handed the card back to me. She did not even look inside.

"Not this year," she said.

"Why not this year?"

"Sophie, it is not mine. It is your mother's. We must send it to your mother."

I only knew my mother from the picture on the night table by Tante Atie's pillow. She waved from inside the frame with a wide grin on her face and a large flower in her hair. She witnessed everything that went on in the bougainvillea, each step, each stumble, each hug and kiss. She saw us when we got up, when we went to sleep, when we laughed, when we got upset at each other. Her expression never changed. Her grin never went away.

I sometimes saw my mother in my dreams. She would chase me through a field of wildflowers as tall as the sky. When she caught me, she would try to squeeze me into the small frame so I could be in the picture with her. I would scream and scream until my voice gave out, then Tante Atie would come and save me from her grasp.

I slipped the card back in my pocket and got up to go inside. Tante Atie lowered her head and covered her face with her hands. Her fingers muffled her voice as she spoke.

"When I am done feeling bad, I will come in and we will find you a very nice envelope for your card. Maybe it will get

8

to your mother after the fact, but she will welcome it because it will come directly from you."

"It is your card," I insisted.

"It is for a mother, your mother." She motioned me away with a wave of her hand. "When it is Aunt's Day, you can make me one."

"Will you let me read it to you?"

"It is not for me to hear, my angel. It is for your mother."

I put the card back in my pocket, plucked out the flower, and dropped it under my shoes.

Across the road, the children were yelling each other's names, inviting passing friends to join them. They sat in a circle and shot the crackling leaves high above their heads. The leaves landed on their faces and clung to their hair. It was almost as though they were caught in a rain of daffodils.

I continued to watch the children as Tante Atie prepared what she was bringing to the potluck. She put the last touches on a large tray of sweet potato pudding that filled the whole house with its molasses scent.

As soon as the sun set, lamps were lit all over our quarter. The smaller children sat playing marbles near whatever light they could find. The older boys huddled in small groups near the school yard fence as they chatted over their books. The girls formed circles around their grandmothers' feet, learning to sew.

Tante Atie had promised that in another year or so she would teach me how to sew.

"You should not stare," she said as we passed a near-sighted old woman whispering mystical secrets of needle and thread to a little girl. The girl was squinting as her eyes dashed back and forth to keep up with the movements of her grandmother's old fingers.

"Can I start sewing soon?" I asked Tante Atie.

"Soon as I have a little time," she said.

She put her hand on my shoulder and bent down to kiss my cheek.

"Is something troubling you?" I asked.

"Don't let my troubles upset you," she said.

"When I made the card, I thought it would make you happy. I did not mean to make you sad."

"You have never done anything to make me sad," she said. "That is why this whole thing is going to be so hard."

A cool evening breeze circled the dust around our feet.

"You should put on your blouse with the long sleeves," she said. "So you don't catch cold."

I wanted to ask her what was going to be so hard, but she pressed her finger over my lips and pointed towards the house.

She said "Go" and so I went.

One by one the men began to file out of their houses. Some carried plantains, others large Negro yams, which made your body itch if you touched them raw. There were no men in Tante Atie's and my house so we carried the food ourselves to the yard where the children had been playing.

The women entered the yard with tins of steaming ginger tea and baskets of cassava bread. Tante Atie and I sat near the gate, she behind the women and me behind the girls.

Monsieur Augustin stacked some twigs with a rusty pitchfork and dropped his ripe plantains and husked corn on the pile. He lit a long match and dropped it on the top of the heap. The flame spread from twig to twig, until they all blended into a large smoky fire.

Monsieur Augustin's wife began to pass around large cups of ginger tea. The men broke down into small groups and strolled down the garden path, smoking their pipes. Old *tantes*—aunties—and grandmothers swayed cooing babies on their laps. The teenage boys and girls drifted to dark corners, hidden by the shadows of rustling banana leaves.

Tante Atie said that the way these potlucks started was really a long time ago in the hills. Back then, a whole village would get together and clear a field for planting. The group would take turns clearing each person's land, until all the land in the village was cleared and planted. The women would cook large amounts of food while the men worked. Then at sunset, when the work was done, everyone would gather together and enjoy a feast of eating, dancing, and laughter.

Here in Croix-des-Rosets, most of the people were city workers who labored in baseball or clothing factories and lived in small cramped houses to support their families back in the provinces. Tante Atie said that we were lucky to live in a house as big as ours, with a living room to receive our guests, plus a room for the two of us to sleep in. Tante Atie said that only people living on New York money or people with professions, like Monsieur Augustin, could afford to live in a house where they did not have to share a yard with a pack of other people. The others had to live in huts, shacks, or one-room houses that, sometimes, they had to build themselves.

In spite of where they might live, this potluck was open to

everybody who wanted to come. There was no field to plant, but the workers used their friendships in the factories or their grouping in the common yards as a reason to get together, eat, and celebrate life.

Tante Atie kept looking at Madame Augustin as she passed the tea to each person in the women's circle around us.

"How is Martine?" Madame Augustin handed Tante Atie a cup of steaming tea. Tante Atie's hand jerked and the tea sprinkled the back of Madame Augustin's hand.

"I saw the *facteur* bring you something big yesterday." Madame Augustin blew into her tea as she spoke. "Did your sister send you a gift?"

Tante Atie tried to ignore the question.

"Was it a gift?" insisted Madame Augustin. "It is not the child's birthday again, is it? She was just twelve, no less than two months ago."

I wondered why Tante Atie had not showed me the big package. Usually, my mother would send us two cassettes with our regular money allowance. One cassette would be for me and Tante Atie, the other for my grandmother. Usually, Tante Atie and I would listen to our cassette together. Maybe she was saving it for later.

I tried to listen without looking directly at the women's faces. That would have been disrespectful, as bad as speaking without being spoken to.

"How is Martine doing over there?" asked Stéphane, the albino's wife. She was a sequins piece worker, who made herself hats from leftover factory sequins. That night she was wearing a gold bonnet that make her look like a star had landed on her head.

"My sister is fine, thank you," Tante Atie finally answered.

Madame Augustin took a sip of her tea and looked over at me. She gave me a reprimanding look that said: Why aren't you playing with the other children? I quickly lowered my eyes, pretending to be studying some random pebbles on the ground.

"I would wager that it is very nice over there in New York," Madame Augustin said.

"I suppose it could be," said Tante Atie.

"Why have you never gone?" asked Madame Augustin.

"Perhaps it is not yet the time," said Tante Atie.

"Perhaps it is," corrected Madame Augustin.

She leaned over Tante Atie's shoulder and whispered in a not so low voice, "When are you going to tell us, Atie, when the car comes to take you to the airplane?"

"Is Martine sending for you?" asked the albino's wife.

Suddenly, all the women began to buzz with questions.

"When are you leaving?"

"Can it really be as sudden as that?"

"Will you marry there?"

"Will you remember us?"

"I am not going anywhere," Tante Atie interrupted.

"I have it on good information that it was a plane ticket that you received the other day," said Madame Augustin. "If you are not going, then who was the plane ticket for?"

All their eyes fell on me at the same time.

"Is the mother sending for the child?" asked the albino's wife.

13

"I saw the delivery," said Madame Augustin.

"Then she is sending for the child," they concluded.

Suddenly a large hand was patting my shoulder.

"This is very good news," said the accompanying voice. "It is the best thing that is ever going to happen to you."

I could not eat the bowl of food that Tante Atie laid in front of me. I only kept wishing that everyone would disappear so I could go back home.

The night very slowly slipped into the early hours of the morning. Soon everyone began to drift towards their homes. On Saturdays there was the house to clean and water to fetch from long distances and the clothes to wash and iron for the Mother's Day Mass.

After everyone was gone, Monsieur Augustin walked Tante Atie and me home. When we got to our door he moved closer to Tante Atie as though he wanted to whisper something in her ear. She looked up at him and smiled, then quickly covered her lips with her fingers, as though she suddenly remembered her missing teeth and did not want him to see them.

He turned around to look across the street. His wife was carrying some of the pots back inside the house. He squeezed Tante Atie's hand and pressed his cheek against hers.

"It is good news, Atie," he said. "Neither you nor Sophie should be sad. A child belongs with her mother, and a mother with her child."

His wife was now sitting on the steps in front of their bougainvillea, waiting for him.

"I did not think you would tell your wife before I had a chance to tell the child," said Tante Atie to Monsieur Augustin.

"You must be brave," he said. "It is some very wonderful news for this child."

The night had grown a bit cool, but we both stood and watched as Monsieur Augustin crossed the street, took the pails from his wife's hand and bent down to kiss her forehead. He put his arms around her and closed the front door behind them.

"When you tell someone something and you call it a secret, they should know not to tell others," Tante Atie mumbled to herself.

She kept her eyes on the Augustin's house. The main light in their bedroom was lit. Their bodies were silhouetted on the ruffled curtains blowing in the night breeze. Monsieur Augustin sat in a rocking chair by the window. His wife sat on his lap as she unlaced her long braid of black hair. Monsieur Augustin brushed the hair draped like a silk blanket down Madame Augustin's back. When he was done, Monsieur Augustin got up to undress. Then slowly, Madame Augustin took off her day clothes and slipped into a long-sleeved night gown. Their laughter rose in the night as they began a tickling fight. The light flickered off and they tumbled into bed.

Tante Atie kept looking at the window even after all signs of the Augustins had faded into the night.

A tear rolled down her cheek as she unbolted the door to go inside. I immediately started walking towards our bedroom. She raced after me and tried to catch up. When she did, she pressed her hand down on my shoulder and tried to turn my body around, to face her.

"Do you know why I always wished I could read?"

Her teary eyes gazed directly into mine.

"I don't know why." I tried to answer as politely as I could.

"It was always my dream to read," she said, "so I could read that old Bible under my pillow and find the answers to everything right there between those pages. What do you think that old Bible would have us do right now, about this moment?"

"I don't know," I said.

"How can you not know?" she asked. "You try to tell me there is all wisdom in reading but at a time like this you disappoint me."

"You lied!" I shouted.

She grabbed both my ears and twisted them until they burned.

I stomped my feet and walked away. As I rushed to bed, I began to take off my clothes so quickly that I almost tore them off my body.

The smell of lemon perfume stung my nose as I pulled the sheet over my head.

"I did not lie," she said, "I kept a secret, which is different. I wanted to tell you. I needed time to reconcile myself, to accept it. It was very sudden, just a cassette from Martine saying, 'I want my daughter,' and then as fast as you can put two fingers together to snap, she sends me a plane ticket with a date on it. I am not even certain that she is doing this properly. All she tells me is that she arranged it with a woman who works on the airplane."

"Was I ever going to know?" I asked.

"I was going to put you to sleep, put you in a suitcase, and send you to her. One day you would wake up there and you would feel like your whole life here with me was a dream." She tried to force a laugh, but it didn't make it past her throat. "I had this plan, you see. I thought it was a good plan. I was going to tell you this, that in one week you would be going to see your mother. As far as you would know, it would just be a visit. I felt it in my heart and took it on Monsieur Augustin's advice that, once you got there, you would love it so much that you would beg your mother to let you stay. You have heard with your own two ears what everyone has said. We have no right to be sad."

I sunk deeper and deeper into the bed and lost my body in the darkness, in the folds of the sheets.

The bed creaked loudly as Tante Atie climbed up on her side.

"Don't you ever tell anyone that I cry when I watch Donald and his wife getting ready for bed," she said, sobbing.

I groped for my clothes in the dark and found the Mother's Day card I had made her. I tucked it under her pillow as I listened to her mumble some final words in her sleep.

Chapter 2

ᐱᐱᐱᐱᐱᐱᐱᐱ

The smell of cinnamon rice pudding scented the whole kitchen. Tante Atie was sitting at the table with a bowl in front of her when I came in. I felt closer to tears with each word I even thought of saying, so I said nothing.

I sat at my usual place at the table and watched out of the corner of my eyes as she poured a bowl of rice pudding and slid it towards me.

"*Bonjou*," she said, waving a spoon in front of my face. "Your *bonjou*, your greeting, is your passport."

I kept my head down and took the spoon only when she laid it down in front of me. I did not feel like eating, but if I did not eat, we would have had to sit and stare at one another, and sooner or later, one of us would have had to say something.

I picked up the spoon and began to eat. Tante Atie's lips

spread into a little grin as she watched me. Her laughter prefaced the start of what was going to be a funny story.

There were many stories that Tante Atie liked to tell. There were mostly sad stories, but every once in a while, there was a funny one. There was the time when she was a little girl, when my grandmother was a practicing Protestant. Grandmè Ifé tried to show her Christian faith by standing over the edge of a snake pit and ordering the devils back into the ground. Tante Atie was always bent over with laughter as she remembered the look on Grandmè Ifé's face when one of the snakes started to crawl up the side of the pit towards her. My grandmother did not come out for days after that.

Whether something was funny or not depended on the way Tante Atie told it. That morning, she could not bring the laughter out of me like she had in the past. It was even hard for her to force it out of herself.

After I had eaten, I washed the dishes and put them in the basket to dry.

"I want to tell you a few things," Tante Atie said from where she was sitting at the table. "You need to know certain things about your mother."

"Why can't you come to New York too?" I interrupted.

"Because it is not the time yet. After you leave, I am going back home to take care of your grandmother. I am only here in Croix-des-Rosets because of your schooling. Once you leave, I can go back."

"I don't know why you can't go to New York too," I said.

"We are each going to our mothers. That is what was supposed to happen. Your mother wants to see you now, Sophie. She does not want you to forget who your *real* mother is. When she left you with me, she and I, we agreed that it would only be for a while. You were just a baby then. She left you because she was going to a place she knew nothing about. She did not want to take chances with you."

Tante Atie opened the front door and let the morning sun inside. She ran her fingers along the grilled iron as she looked up at the clear indigo sky.

She picked up a broom and began to sweep the mosaic floor.

"My angel," she said, "I would like to know that by word or by example I have taught you love. I must tell you that I do love your mother. Everything I love about you, I loved in her first. That is why I could never fight her about keeping you here. I do not want you to go and fight with her either. In this country, there are many good reasons for mothers to abandon their children." She stopped to pound the dust out of the living room cushions. "But you were never abandoned. You were with me. Your mother and I, when we were children we had no control over anything. Not even this body." She pounded her fist over her chest and stomach. "When my father died, my mother had to dig a hole and just drop him in it. We are a family with dirt under our fingernails. Do you know what that means?"

She did not wait for me to answer.

"That means we've worked the land. We're not *educated*. My father would have never dreamt that we would live in the same kind of house that people like Monsieur and Madame Augustin live in. He, a school teacher, and we, daughters of the hills, old peasant stock, *pitit soyèt*, ragamuffins. If we can live here, if you have this door open to you, it is because of your mother. Promise me that you are not going to fight with your mother when you get there."

"I am not going to fight," I said.

"Good," she said. "It would be a shame if the two of you got into battles because you share a lot more than you know."

She reached over and touched the collar of my lemon-toned house dress.

"Everything you own is yellow," she said, "wildflower yellow, like dandelions, sunflowers."

"And daffodils," I added.

"That is right," she said, "your mother, she loved daffodils." Tante Atie told me that my mother loved daffodils because they grew in a place that they were not supposed to. They were really European flowers, French buds and stems, meant for colder climates. A long time ago, a French woman had brought them to Croix-des-Rosets and planted them there. A strain of daffodils had grown that could withstand the heat, but they were the color of pumpkins and golden summer squash, as though they had acquired a bronze tinge from the skin of the natives who had adopted them.

Tante Atie took the card from under her pillow and put it on the night table, next to the plane ticket. She said that it would be nice for me to give the card to my mother personally, even though the daffodil was gone.

Chapter 3

/\/\/\/\/\/\/\/\

The trip to La Nouvelle Dame Marie took five hours in a rocky van. However, Tante Atie thought that I couldn't leave for New York without my grandmother's blessing. Besides, Grandmè Ifé was getting on in years and this could be my last chance to see her.

The van from Croix-des-Rosets let us off in the marketplace in Dame Marie. The roads to my grandmother's house were too rough for anything but wheelbarrows, mules, or feet.

Tante Atie and I decided to go on foot. We walked by a line of thatched huts where a group of women were pounding millet in a large mortar with a pestle. Others were cooking large cassava cakes in flat pans over charcoal pits.

In the cane fields, the men chopped cane stalks as they sang back and forth to one another. A crammed wheelbarrow rolled towards us. We stepped aside and allowed the boys to pass. They were bare-chested and soaked with sweat, with no protection from the sun except old straw hats.

We passed a farm with a bamboo fence around it. The owner was Man Grace, a tall woman who had hair patches growing out of her chin. Man Grace and her daughter were working in the yard, throwing handfuls of purple corn at a flock of guinea fowls.

My mother had sent money for the reconstruction of her old home. The house stood out from all the others in Dame Marie. It was a flat red brick house with wide windows and a shingled roof. A barbed wire fence bordered my grandmother's pumpkin vines and tuberose stems.

I raced up to the front of the house to stand under the rooster-shaped weather vanes spinning on my grandmother's porch. My grandmother was in the yard, pulling a rope out of her stone well.

"Old woman, I brought your child," Tante Atie said.

The rope slipped out of my grandmother's hands, the bucket crashing with an echoing splash. I leaped into her arms, nearly knocking her down.

"It does my heart a lot of good to see you," she said.

Tante Atie kissed my grandmother on the cheek and then went inside the house.

Grandmè Ifé wrapped her arms around my body. Her head came up to my chin, her mop of shrubby white hair tickling my lips.

"Are you hungry?" she asked. "I am going to cook only the things you like."

. . .

At night, the huts on the hills looked like a crowd of candles. We ate supper on the back porch. My grandmother cooked rice and Congo beans with sun-dried mushrooms. She was wearing a long black dress, as part of her *deuil*, to mourn my grandfather.

"Tell me, what good things have you been doing?" asked my grandmother.

"She has been getting all the highest marks in school," said Tante Atie. "Her mother will be very proud."

"You must never forget this," said my grandmother. "Your mother is your first friend."

I slept alone in the third room in the house. It had a large four-poster bed and a mahogany wardrobe with giant hibiscus carved all over it. The mattress sank as I slipped under the sheets in the bed. It was nice to have a bed of my own every so often.

I lay in bed, waiting for the nightmare where my mother would finally get to take me away.

We left the next day to return to Croix-des-Rosets. Tante Atie had to go back to work. Besides, my grandmother said that it was best that we leave before she got too used to us and suffered a sudden attack of chagrin.

To my grandmother, chagrin was a genuine physical disease. Like a hurt leg or a broken arm. To treat chagrin, you drank tea from leaves that only my grandmother and other old wise women could recognize.

We each gave my grandmother two kisses as she urged us to go before she kept us for good.

"Can one really die of chagrin?" I asked Tante Atie in the van on the way back.

She said it was not a sudden illness, but something that could kill you slowly, taking a small piece of you every day until one day it finally takes all of you away.

"How can we keep it from happening to us?" I asked.

"We don't choose it," she said, "it chooses us. A horse has four legs, but it can fall anyway."

She told me about a group of people in Guinea who carry the sky on their heads. They are the people of Creation. Strong, tall, and mighty people who can bear anything. Their Maker, she said, gives them the sky to carry because they are strong. These people do not know who they are, but if you see a lot of trouble in your life, it is because you were chosen to carry part of the sky on your head.

Chapter 4

/\/\/\/\/\/\/\/\

That whole week, Tante Atie left for work before dawn and came home very late at night. She left me food to eat and asked Monsieur Augustin to stop by in the mornings and evenings to check on me. When she came home, I watched, through the faint ray of light that crept across the sheet, as she tiptoed over to our bed, before going to sleep. That was how I knew for sure that she had not run away and left me.

I went to school every day as usual. After school, I went into our yard and spent the afternoons gathering the twigs and leaves that kept it from being clean.

When I came home from school Friday afternoon, I saw Tante Atie sitting on the steps in front of the bougainvillea. When she saw me, she ran towards me and swept my body in the air.

"You cleaned up real good," she said.

I had done my last cleaning that morning, before leaving for school. The dead leaves were stacked on top of fallen branches, twigs, and dried flowers.

Tante Atie kissed both my cheeks and carried my notebook inside. The living room seemed filled by the suitcase that she had bought me for the trip. While I was working on the yard, I had somehow told myself that I would be around for more potlucks, more trips to my grandmother's, even a sewing lesson. The suitcase made me realize that I would never get to do those things.

"I know I have not been here all week," Tante Atie said. "I wanted to work extra hours to get you some gifts for your trip."

She poured hot milk from a silver kettle that she had always kept on the shelf for display. Stuck to the bottom of the kettle was a small note, *Je t'aime de tout mon coeur*. The note read, "I love you very much." It was signed by Monsieur Augustin.

I reached over to grab the note dangling from the kettle. Tante Atie snatched it back quickly. She held it upside down and looked at it as though it were a picture, fading before her eyes.

She turned her back quickly and placed the note on the shelf.

We sat across the table from one another and drank without saying anything. I tried to hide my tears behind the tea cup.

"No crying," she said. "We are going to be strong as mountains."

The tears had already fallen and hit my cheeks.

"Mountains," she said, prodding my ribs with her elbow.

She bent and picked up a white box from the heap of things that she had bought. Inside was a saffron dress with a large white collar and baby daffodils embroidered all over it.

"This is for you to wear on your trip," she said.

My mother's face was in my dreams all night long. She was wrapped in yellow sheets and had daffodils in her hair. She opened her arms like two long hooks and kept shouting out my name. Catching me by the hem of my dress, she wrestled me to the floor. I called for Tante Atie as loud as I could. Tante Atie was leaning over us, but she could not see me. I was lost in the yellow of my mother's sheets.

I woke up with Tante Atie leaning over my bed. She was already dressed in one of her pink Sunday dresses, and had perfume and face powder on. I walked by her on my way to the wash basin. She squeezed my hand and whispered, "Remember that we are going to be like mountains and mountains don't cry."

"Unless it rains," I said.

"When it rains, it is the sky that is crying."

When I came from the wash basin, she was waiting for me with a towel. It was one of many white towels that she kept in a box under her bed, for special occasions that never came. I used the towel to dry my body, then slipped into the starched underwear and the dress she handed to me.

The suitcase was in a corner in the kitchen. The table was covered with white lace cloth. Tante Atie's special, unused china plates and glasses were filled with oatmeal and milk.

She led me to the head of the table and sat by my side. A slight morning drizzle hit the iron grills on the door.

"If it rains, will I still have to go?" I asked her.

She ran her finger over a shiny scar on the side of her head.

"Yes, you will have to go," she said. "There is nothing we can do to stop that now. I have already asked someone to come and drive us to the *aéroport*."

She took a sip from the milk in her glass and forced a large smile.

"You should not be afraid," she said. "Martine was a wonderful sister. She will be a great mother to you. Crabs don't make papayas. She is my sister."

She reached inside her pocket and pulled out the card that I had made her for Mother's Day. It was very wrinkled now and the penciled words were beginning to fade.

"I would not let you read it to me, but I know it says some very nice things," she said, putting the card next to my plate. "It is not so pretty now, but your mother, she will still love it."

Before she could stop me, I began to read her the words.

> My mother is a daffodil,
> limber and strong as one.
> My mother is a daffodil,
> but in the wind, iron strong.

"You see," Tante Atie shrugged. "it was never for me." She slipped the card in the pocket of my dress. "When you get there, you give that to her."

"She will not be able to see the words," I said.

"She will see them fine and if she cannot see them, you read them to her like you just did for me and from now on, her name is *Manman*.

Chabin, the lottery agent, peeked his head through the open door, waving his record book at us.

"We do not want to play today," Tante Atie said.

"I am here to pay you," Chabin said. "Don't you follow the results? Your number, it came out. You are a winner."

Tante Atie looked very happy.

"How much did I win?" she asked.

"Ten *gourdes*," he said.

He counted out the money and handed it to her.

"You see," Tante Atie said, clutching her money. "Your mother, she brings me luck."

The Peugeot taxi came for us while we were still at the table. I left Tante Atie's kitchen, my breakfast uneaten and the dishes undone.

The drizzle had stopped. The neighbors were watching as the driver carried my one suitcase to the car.

The Augustins came over to say good-bye. Madame Augustin slipped a crisp pink handkerchief in my hand as she kissed me four times—twice on each cheek.

"If you study hard, you will have no trouble with your English," Monsieur Augustin said as he firmly shook my hand.

I held Tante Atie's hand as we climbed into the back seat. Our faces were dry, our heads up. We were like sunflowers, staring directly at the sun.

Before pulling away, the driver turned his head and complimented us on our very clean yard.

"My child, she cleans it," Tante Atie said.

The car scattered the neighbors and the factory workers, as they waved a group farewell. Maybe if I had a really good friend my eyes would have clung to hers as we were driven away. A red dust rose between me and the only life that I had ever known. There were no children playing, no leaves flying about. No daffodils.

Chapter 5

∧∧∧∧∧∧∧∧∧

The sun crawled across our faces as the car sped into Port-au-Prince. I had never been to the city before. Colorful boutiques with neon signs lined the street. Vans covered with pictures of flowers and horses with wings scurried up and down and made sudden stops in the middle of the boulevards.

Tante Atie gasped each time we went by a large department store or a towering hotel. She shouted the names of places that she had visited in years past.

When they were teenagers, she and my mother would save their pennies all year long so they could come to the city on Christmas Eve. They would tell my grandmother that they were traveling with one of the old peddlers, but that was never their plan. They would take a *tap tap* van in the afternoon so as to arrive in Port-au-Prince just as the sun was setting, and the Christmas lights were beginning to glow.

They stood outside the stores in their Sunday dresses to listen to the sounds of the toy police cars and talking dolls chattering over the festive music. They went to Mass at the Gothic cathedral, then spent the rest of the night sitting by the fountains and gazing at the Nativity scenes on the Champs-de-Mars. They bought ice cream cones and fireworks, while young tourists offered them cigarettes for the privilege of taking their pictures. They pretended to be students at one of the gentry's universities and even went so far as describing the plush homes they said they lived in. The white tourists flirted with them and held their hands. They laughed at silly jokes, letting their voices rise and fall like city girls. Later, they made rendezvous for the next night, which of course they never kept. Then before dawn, they took a van back home and slipped into bed before my grandmother woke up.

I looked outside and saw the bare hills that bordered the national highway.

"We are almost there," the driver said as he slowed down, almost to a stop.

We waited for a while for the car to move.

"Is there some trouble?" asked Tante Atie.

"There is always some trouble here," the driver said. "They are changing the name of the airport from François Duvalier to Maïs Gaté, like it was before François Duvalier was president."

Tante Atie's body tensed up.

"Did they have to do it today?" Tante Atie asked. "She will be delayed. We cannot miss our appointment."

33

"I will do what I can," the driver said, "but some things are beyond our control."

I moved closer to the window to get a better look. Clouds of sooty smoke were rising to the sky from a place not too far ahead.

"I think there is a fire," the driver said.

Tante Atie pushed her head forward and tried to see.

"Maybe the world, it is ending," she said.

We began to move slowly in a long line of cars. Dark green army vans passed through narrow spaces between cars. The driver followed the slow-paced line. Soon we were at the airport gate.

We stopped in front of the main entrance. The smoke had been coming from across the street. Army trucks surrounded a car in flames. A group of students were standing on top of a hill, throwing rocks at the burning car. They scurried to avoid the tear gas and the round of bullets that the soldiers shot back at them.

Some of the students fell and rolled down the hill. They screamed at the soldiers that they were once again betraying the people. One girl rushed down the hill and grabbed one of the soldiers by the arm. He raised his pistol and pounded it on top of her head. She fell to the ground, her face covered with her own blood.

Tante Atie grabbed my shoulder and shoved me quickly inside the airport gate.

"Do you see what you are leaving?" she said.

"I know I am leaving you."

The airport lobby was very crowded. We tried to keep up with the driver as he ran past the vendors and travelers, dragging my suitcase behind him.

As we waited on the New York boarding line, Tante Atie and I looked up at the paintings looming over us from the ceiling. There were pictures of men and women pulling carts and selling rice and beans to make some money.

A woman shouted "Madame," drawing us out of the visions above us. She looked breathless, as though she had been searching for us for a long time.

"You are Sophie Caco?" she asked, speaking directly to me.

I nodded.

Tante Atie looked at her lean body and her neat navy uniform and hesitated before shaking her hand.

"I will take good care of her," she said to Tante Atie in Creole. She immediately took my hand. "Her mother is going to meet her in New York. I spoke to her this morning. Everything is arranged. We cannot waste time."

Tante Atie's lips quivered.

"We have to go now," the lady said. "You were very tardy."

"We were not at fault," Tante Atie tried to explain.

"It does not matter now," the lady said. "We must go."

Tante Atie bent down and pressed her cheek against mine.

"Say hello to your manman for me," she said. "You must not concern yourself about me."

The driver tapped Tante Atie's shoulder.

"There could be some more chaos," he said. "I want to go before things become very bad."

"Don't you worry yourself about me," Tante Atie said. "I am not going to be lonely. I will be with your grandmother. Just you always remember how much your Tante Atie loves and cherishes you."

35

The woman tugged at my hand.

"We really must go," she said.

"She is going," Tante Atie said, releasing my hand.

The woman started walking away. I moved along with her taking big steps to keep up. I kept turning my head and waving at Tante Atie. Her large body stood out in the middle of the airport lobby.

People rubbed against her as they rushed past. She stood in the same spot wiping her tears with a patchwork handkerchief. In her pink dress and brown sandals, with the village dust settled on her toes, it was easy to tell that she did not belong there. She blended in neither with the smiling well-dressed groups on their way to board the planes nor with the jeans-clad tourists whom the panhandlers surrounded at the gate.

She stood by the exit gate and watched as the woman pulled me though a glass door onto the runway leading to the plane.

The plane was nearly full. There were only a few empty seats. I followed the woman down the narrow aisle. She showed me to a seat by a window. I slipped in quickly and looked outside, hoping to see Tante Atie heading safely home.

I only saw a patch of the smoky sky. The woman left. She soon came back with a little boy. He was crying and stomping his feet, struggling to wiggle out of her grasp. She cornered him against the seats and pressed him into the chair. She held him down with both her hands. He stopped fighting, slid upward in the seat, raised his head, and spat in her face.

His shirt was soaked with the saliva that was still dripping from either side of his mouth. He rubbed his already-red eyes with the back of his hand. Leaning forward, he pressed his face against the seat in front of him. It was almost as though he was trying to find a way to muffle his own sobs.

I reached over to stroke his head. He grabbed my hand and dug his teeth into my fingers. I hit his arm and tried to get him to release my fingers. He bit even harder. I smacked his shoulder. He let go of my fingers and began to scream.

The woman rushed over. She pulled him from the seat, raised him up to her chest, and rocked him in her arms. He clung to her body for a moment then pulled away, digging his fingers into her neck. She stumbled backwards and nearly fell. He slipped out of her arms and ran out of her reach. She dashed down the aisle after him.

A tall man blocked the aisle and stood in the little boy's way. He began to cry louder when he noticed that he was cornered. He jumped on a passenger's lap and began to pound his head on a side window. The man grabbed him and wrestled him back to his seat. He strapped him down with his seatbelt, then leaned over and did the same for me.

As soon as his seatbelt was on, the boy sat still. Both the man and the woman stood over him and watched him carefully, as though they were expecting him to reach up and grab one of their eyeballs. He did nothing. He sat back in his seat, bent his head, and wept silently.

"What is the matter with him?" the man said in French.

"His father died in that fire out front. His father was some kind of old government official, très corrupt," she whispered. "Très guilty of crimes against the people."

"And we are letting him travel?"

"He does not have any more relatives here. His father's sister lives in New York. I called her. She is going to meet him there."

"I can see why he is upset," the man said.

The plane began to roar towards the sky. I looked outside and saw the cars heading away. I could not tell Tante Atie's taxi from the others.

The sound of the engine silenced the boy's sobs. He soon fell asleep, and shortly after, so did I.

Chapter 6

⋀⋁⋀⋁⋀⋁⋀⋁

"Children, we are here." The woman was shaking both of us at the same time.

The plane was empty. We walked down a long passageway, the woman first, with the little boy's hand in hers, and then me. She rushed us by the different lines without stopping. She only waved each time and flashed a large manila envelope.

We soon joined a crowd and watched as suitcases filed past us on a moving mat.

"Do you see your bags?" she asked.

I saw my suitcase and pointed to it. She walked over and picked it up and put it on the floor next to me. We waited for the little boy to point out his, but he did not.

She leafed through his papers and said, "Jean-Claude, do you see your suitcase?"

He buried his face in her skirt and began to cry. She

walked over and checked the stubs on the suitcases. He did not have any.

We walked down another corridor. Then a glass gate opened itself and we were out in a lobby filled with people holding balloons and flowers. Some of them burst forward to hug loved ones.

A woman moaned as she walked towards Jean-Claude. She grabbed him and squeezed his little body against hers.

"They've killed my brother," she cried. "Look at him, look at my brother's son."

She carried him away in her arms, his face buried in her chest.

My mother came forward. I knew it was my mother because she came up to me and grabbed me and begin to spin me like a top, so she could look at me.

The woman who had been with me looked on without saying anything.

"Stay here," my mother said to me in Creole.

She walked over to a corner with the woman, whispered a few things to her, and handed her what seemed like money.

"I cannot thank you enough," my mother said.

"There is no need," the woman said. She bowed slightly and walked away.

I raised my hand to wave good-bye. The woman had already turned her back and was heading inside. It was as though I had disappeared. She did not even see me anymore.

As the woman went through the gate, my mother kissed me on the lips.

"I cannot believe that I am looking at you," she said. "You are my little girl. You are here."

She pinched my cheeks and patted my head.

"Say something," she urged. "Say something. Just speak to me. Let me hear your voice."

She pressed my face against hers and held fast.

"How are you feeling?" she asked. "Did you have a nice plane flight?"

I nodded.

"You must be very tired," she said. "Let us go home."

She grabbed my suitcase with one hand and my arm with the other.

Outside it was overcast and cool.

"My goodness." Her scrawny body shivered. "I didn't even bring you something to put over your dress."

She dropped the suitcase on the sidewalk, took off the denim jacket she had on and guided my arms through the sleeves.

A line of cars stopped as we crossed the street to the parking lot. She was wobbling under the weight of my suitcase.

She stopped in front of a pale yellow car with a long crack across the windshield glass. The paint was peeling off the side door that she opened for me. I peered inside and hesitated to climb onto the tattered cushions on the seats.

She dropped the suitcase in the trunk and walked back to me.

"Don't be afraid. Go right in."

She tried to lift my body into the front seat but she stumbled under my weight and quickly put me back down.

I climbed in and tried not to squirm. The sharp edge of a loose spring was sticking into my thigh.

She sat in the driver's seat and turned on the engine. It made a loud grating noise as though it were about to explode.

"We will soon be on our way," she said.

She rubbed her hands together and pressed her head back against the seat. She did not look like the picture Tante Atie had on her night table. Her face was long and hollow. Her hair had a blunt cut and she had long spindly legs. She had dark circles under her eyes and, as she smiled, lines of wrinkles tightened her expression. Her fingers were scarred and sunburned. It was as though she had never stopped working in the cane fields after all.

"It is ready now," she said.

She strapped the seatbelt across her flat chest, pressing herself even further into the torn cushions. She leaned over and attached my seatbelt as the car finally drove off.

Night had just fallen. Lights glowed everywhere. A long string of cars sped along the highway, each like a single diamond on a very long bracelet.

"We will be in the city soon," she said.

I still had not said anything to her.

"How is your Tante Atie?" she asked. "Does she still go to night school?"

"Night school?"

"She told me once in a cassette that she was going to start night school. Did she ever start it?"

"Non."

"The old girl lost her nerve. She lost her fight. You should have seen us when we were young. We always dreamt of becoming important women. We were going to be the first women doctors from my mother's village. We would not stop at being doctors either. We were going to be engineers too. Imagine our surprise when we found out we had limits."

All the street lights were suddenly gone. The streets we drove down now were dim and hazy. The windows were draped with bars; black trash bags blew out into the night air.

There were young men standing on street corners, throwing empty cans at passing cars. My mother swerved the car to avoid a bottle that almost came crashing through the windshield.

"How is Lotus?" she asked. "Donald's wife, Madame Augustin."

"She is fine," I said.

"Atie has sent me cassettes about that. You know Lotus was not meant to marry Donald. Your aunt Atie was supposed to. But the heart is fickle, what can you say? When Lotus came along, he did not want my sister anymore."

There was writing all over the building. As we walked towards it, my mother nearly tripped over a man sleeping under a blanket of newspapers.

"Your schooling is the only thing that will make people respect you," my mother said as she put a key in the front door.

The thick dirty glass was covered with names written in graffiti bubbles.

"You are going to work hard here," she said, "and no one is going to break your heart because you cannot read or write. You have a chance to become the kind of woman Atie and I have always wanted to be. If you make something of yourself in life, we will all succeed. You can *raise our heads*."

A smell of old musty walls met us at the entrance to her apartment. She closed the door behind her and dragged the suitcase inside.

"You wait for me here," she said, once we got inside. I stood on the other side of a heavy door in the dark hall, waiting for her.

She disappeared behind a bedroom door. I wandered in and slid my fingers across the table and chairs neatly lined up in the kitchen. The tablecloth was shielded with a red plastic cover, the same blush red as the sofa in the living room.

There were books scattered all over the counter. I flipped through the pages quickly. The books had pictures of sick old people in them and women dressed in white helping them.

I was startled to hear my name when she called it.

"Sophie, where are you?"

I ran back to the spot where she had left me. She was standing there with a tall well-dressed doll at her side. The doll was caramel-colored with a fine pointy noise.

"Come," she said. "We will show you to your room."

I followed her through a dark doorway. She turned on the light and laid the doll down on a small day-bed by the window.

I kept my eyes on the blue wallpaper and the water stains that crept from the ceiling down to the floor.

She kept staring at my face for a reaction.

"Don't you like it?" she asked.

"Yes. I like it. Thank you."

Sitting on the edge of the bed, she unbraided the doll's hair, taking out the ribbons and barrettes that matched the yellow dress. She put them on a night table near the bed. There was a picture of her and Tante Atie there. Tante Atie was holding a baby and my mother had her hand around Tante Atie's shoulder.

I moved closer to get a better look at the baby in Tante Atie's arms. I had never seen an infant picture of myself, but somehow I knew that it was me. Who else could it have been? I looked for traces in the child, a feature that was my mother's but still mine too. It was the first time in my life that I noticed that I looked like no one in my family. Not my mother. Not my Tante Atie. I did not look like them when I was a baby and I did not look like them now.

"If you don't like the room," my mother said, "we can always change it."

She glanced at the picture as she picked up a small brush and combed the doll's hair into a ponytail.

"I like the room fine," I stuttered.

She tied a rubber band around the doll's ponytail, then reached under the bed for a small trunk.

She unbuttoned the back of the doll's dress and changed her into a pajama set.

"You won't resent sharing your room, will you?" She stroked the doll's back. "She is like a friend to me. She kept me company while we were apart. It seems crazy, I know. A grown woman like me with a doll. I am giving her to you now. You take good care of her."

She motioned for me to walk over and sit on her lap. I was not sure that her thin legs would hold me without snapping. I walked over and sat on her lap anyway.

"You're not going to be alone," she said. "I'm never going to be farther than a few feet away. Do you understand that?"

She gently helped me down from her lap. Her knees seemed to be weakening under my weight.

"Do you want to eat something? We can sit and talk. Or do you want to go to bed?"

"Bed."

She reached over to unbutton the back of my dress.

"I can do that," I said.

"Do you want me to show you where I sleep, in case you need me during the night?"

We went back to the living room. She unfolded the sofa and turned it into a bed.

"This is where I'll be. You see, I'm not far away at all."

When we went back to the bedroom, I turned my back to her as I undressed. She took the dress from me, opened the closet door, and squeezed it in between some of her own.

The rumpled Mother's Day card was sticking out from my dress pocket.

"What is that?" she asked, pulling it out.

She unfolded the card and began to read it. I lay down on the bed and tried to slip under the yellow sheets. There was not enough room for both me and the doll on the bed. I picked her up and laid her down sideways. She still left little room for me.

My mother looked up from the card, walked over, and

took the doll out of the bed. She put her down carefully in a corner.

"Was that for me?" she asked looking down at the card.

"Tante Atie said I should give it to you."

"Did you know how much I loved daffodils when I was a girl?"

"Tante Atie told me."

She ran her fingers along the cardboard, over the empty space where the daffodil had been.

"I haven't gone out and looked for daffodils since I've been here. For all I know, they might not even have them here."

She ran the card along her cheek, then pressed it against her chest.

"Are there still lots of daffodils?"

"Oui," I said. "There are a lot of them."

Her face beamed even more than when she first saw me at the airport. She bent down and kissed my forehead.

"Thank God for that," she said.

I couldn't fall asleep. At home, when I couldn't sleep, Tante Atie would stay up with me. The two of us would sit by the window and Tante Atie would tell me stories about our lives, about the way things had been in the family, even before I was born. One time I asked her how it was that I was born with a mother and no father. She told me the story of a little girl who was born out of the petals of roses, water from the stream, and a chunk of the sky. That little girl, she said was me.

As I lay in the dark, I heard my mother talking on the phone.

"Yes," she said in Creole. "She is very much here. In bone and flesh. I cannot believe it myself."

Later that night, I heard that same voice screaming as though someone was trying to kill her. I rushed over, but my mother was alone thrashing against the sheets. I shook her and finally woke her up. When she saw me, she quickly covered her face with her hands and turned away.

"*Ou byen?* Are you all right?" I asked her.

She shook her head yes.

"It is the night," she said. "Sometimes, I see horrible visions in my sleep."

"Do you have any tea you can boil?" I asked.

Tante Atie would have known all the right herbs.

"Don't worry, it will pass," she said, avoiding my eyes. "I will be fine. I always am. The nightmares, they come and go."

There were sirens and loud radios blaring outside the building.

I climbed on the bed and tried to soothe her. She grabbed my face and squeezed it between her palms.

"What is it? Are you scared too?" she asked. "Don't worry." She pulled me down into the bed with her. "You can sleep here tonight if you want. It's okay. I'm here."

She pulled the sheet over both our bodies. Her voice began to fade as she drifted off to sleep.

I leaned back in the bed, listening to her snoring.

Soon, the morning light came creeping through the living room window. I kept staring at the ceiling as I listened to her heart beating along with the ticking clock.

"Sophie," she whispered. Her eyes were still closed. "Sophie, I will never let you go again."

Tears burst out of her eyes when she opened them.

"Sophie, I am glad you are with me. We can get along, you and me. I know we can."

She clung to my hand as she drifted back to sleep.

The sun stung my eyes as it came through the curtains. I slid my hand out of hers to go to the bathroom. The grey linoleum felt surprisingly warm under my feet. I looked at my red eyes in the mirror while splashing cold water over my face. New eyes seemed to be looking back at me. A new face all together. Someone who had aged in one day, as though she had been through a time machine, rather than an airplane. Welcome to New York, this face seemed to be saying. Accept your new life. I greeted the challenge, like one greets a new day. As my mother's daughter and Tante Atie's child.

Chapter 7

/\/\/\/\/\/\/\/\/\

The streets along Flatbush Avenue reminded me of home. My mother took me to Haiti Express, so I could see the place where she sent our money orders and cassettes from.

It was a small room packed with Haitians. People stood on line patiently waiting their turn. My mother slipped Tante Atie's cassette into a padded envelope. As we waited on line, an old fan circled a spider's web above our heads.

A chubby lady greeted my mother politely when we got to the window.

"This is Sophie," my mother said through the holes in the thick glass. "She is the one who has given you so much business over the years."

The lady smiled as she took my mother's money and the package. I kept feeling like there was more I wanted to send to Tante Atie. If I had the power then to shrink myself and slip into the envelope, I would have done it.

I watched as the lady stamped our package and dropped it on top of a larger pile. Around us were dozens of other people trying to squeeze all their love into small packets to send back home.

After we left, my mother stopped at a Haitian beauty salon to buy some castor oil for her hair. Then we went to a small boutique and bought some long skirts and blouses for me to wear to school. My mother said it was important that I learn English quickly. Otherwise, the American students would make fun of me or, even worse, beat me. A lot of other mothers from the nursing home where she worked had told her that their children were getting into fights in school because they were accused of having HBO—Haitian Body Odor. Many of the American kids even accused Haitians of having AIDS because they had heard on television that only the "Four Hs" got AIDS—Heroin addicts, Hemophiliacs, Homosexuals, and Haitians.

I wanted to tell my mother that I didn't want to go to school. Frankly, I was afraid. I tried to think of something to keep me from having to go. Sickness or death were probably the only two things that my mother would accept as excuses.

A car nearly knocked me out of my reverie. My mother grabbed my hand and pulled me across the street. She stopped in front of a pudgy woman selling rice powder and other cosmetics on the street.

"*Sak passé*, Jacqueline?" said my mother.

"You know," answered Jacqueline in Creole. "I'm doing what I can."

Jacqueline was wearing large sponge rollers under a hair net on her head. My mother brought some face cream that promised to make her skin lighter.

All along the avenue were people who seemed displaced among the speeding cars and very tall buildings. They walked and talked and argued in Creole and even played dominoes on their stoops. We found Tante Atie's lemon perfume in a botanica shop. On the walls were earthen jars, tin can lamps, and small statues of the beautiful *mulâtresse*, the goddess and loa Erzulie.

We strolled through long stretches of streets where merengue blared from car windows and children addressed one another in curses.

The outdoor subway tracks seemed to lead to the sky. Pebbles trickled down on us as we crossed under the tracks into another more peaceful neighborhood.

My mother held my hand as we walked through those quiet streets, where the houses had large yards and little children danced around sprinklers on the grass. We stopped in front of a building where the breeze was shaking a sign: MARC CHEVALIER, ESQUIRE.

When my mother rang the bell, a stocky Haitian man came to the door. He was a deep bronze color and very well dressed.

My mother kissed him on the cheek and followed him down a long hallway. On either side of us were bookshelves stacked with large books. My mother let go of my hand as we walked down the corridor. He spoke to her in Creole as he opened the door and let us into his office.

He leaned over and shook my hand.

"Marc Jolibois Francis Legrand Moravien Chevalier."

"*Enchanté*," I said.

I took a deep breath and looked around. On his desk

was a picture of him and my mother, posed against a blue background.

"Are you working late?" my mother asked him.

"Where are you going?" he asked.

"We are just walking around," my mother said. "I am showing her what is where."

"Later, we'll go someplace," he said, patting a folder on his desk.

My mother and I took a bus back to our house. We were crowded and pressed against complete strangers. When we got home, we went through my suitcase and picked out a loose-fitting, high-collared dress Tante Atie had bought me for Sunday Masses. She held it out for me to wear to dinner.

"This is what a proper young lady should wear," she said.

That night, Marc drove us to a restaurant called Miracin's in Asbury Park, New Jersey. The restaurant was at the back of an alley, squeezed between a motel and a dry cleaner.

"Miracin's has the best Haitian food in America," Marc told me as we parked under the motel sign.

"Marc is one of those men who will never recover from not eating his *manman*'s cooking," said my mother. "If he could get her out of her grave to make him dinner, he would do it."

"My mother was the best," Marc said as he opened the car door for us.

There was a tiny lace curtain on the inside of the door. A bell rang as we entered. My mother and I squeezed ourselves between the wall and the table, our bodies wiping the greasy wallpaper clean.

Marc waved to a group of men sitting in a corner loudly talking politics. The room was packed with other customers who shouted back and forth adding their views to the discussion.

"Never the Americans in Haiti again," shouted one man. "Remember what they did in the twenties. They treated our people like animals. They abused the konbit system and they made us work like slaves."

"Roads, we need roads," said another man. "At least they gave us roads. My mother was killed in a ferry accident. If we had roads, we would not need to put crowded boats into the sea, just to go from one small village to another. A lot of you, when you go home, you have to walk from the village to your house, because there are no roads for cars."

"What about the boat people?" added a man from a table near the door. "Because of them, people can't respect us in this country. They lump us all with them."

"All the brains leave the country," Marc said, adding his voice to the mêlée.

"You are insulting the people back home by saying there's no brains there," replied a woman from a table near the back. "There are brains who stay."

"But they are crooks," Marc said, adding some spice to the argument.

"My sister is a nurse there with the Red Cross," said the woman, standing up. "You call that a crook? What have you done for your people?"

For some of us, arguing is a sport. In the marketplace in Haiti, whenever people were arguing, others would gather around them to watch and laugh at the colorful language. People rarely hit each other. They didn't need to. They could wound just as brutally by cursing your mother, calling you a sexual misfit, or accusing you of being from the hills. If you couldn't match them with even stronger accusations, then you would concede the argument by keeping your mouth shut.

Marc decided to stay out of the discussion. The woman continued attacking him, shouting that she was tired of cowardly men speaking against women who were proving themselves, women as brave as stars out at dawn.

My mother smiled at the woman's colorful words. It was her turn to stand up and defend her man, but she said nothing. Marc kept looking at her, as if waiting for my mother to argue on his behalf, but my mother picked up the menu, and ran her fingers down the list of dishes.

My mother introduced me to the waiter when he came by to take her order. He looked at us for a long time. First me, then my mother. I wanted to tell him to stop it. There was no resemblance between us. I knew it.

It was an eternity before we were served. Marc complained about his boudin when it came.

"I can still taste the animal," he said

"What do you expect?" my mother asked. "It is a pig's blood after all."

"It's not well done," he said, while raising the fork to his mouth. "It is an art to make boudin. There is a balance. At best it is a very tight kind of sausage and you would never dream of where it comes from."

"Who taught you to eat this way?" my mother asked.

"Food is a luxury," he said, "but we can not allow ourselves to become gluttons or get fat. Do you hear that, Sophie?"

I shook my head yes, as though I was really very interested. I ate like I had been on a hunger strike, filling myself with the coconut milk they served us in real green coconuts.

When they looked up from their plates, my mother and Marc eyed each other like there were things they couldn't say because of my presence. I tried to stuff myself and keep quiet, pretending that I couldn't even see them. My mother now had two lives: Marc belonged to her present life, I was a living memory from the past.

"What do you want to be when you grow up?" Marc asked me. He spoke to me in a tone of voice that was used with very young children or very old animals.

"I want to do *dactylo*," I said, "be a secretary."

He didn't seem impressed.

"There are a lot of opportunities in this country," he said. "You should reconsider, unless of course this is the passion of your life."

"She is too young now to know," my mother said. "You are going to be a doctor," she told me.

"She still has some time to think," Marc said. "Do you have a boyfriend, Sophie?"

"She is not going to be running wild like those American girls," my mother said. "She will have a boyfriend when she is eighteen."

"And what if she falls in love sooner?" Marc pushed.

"She will put it off until she is eighteen."

We washed down our meal with watermelon juice. Tante Atie always said that eating beets and watermelon would put more red in my blood and give me more strength for hard times.

Chapter 8

∧∨∧∨∧∨∧∨∧∨

School would not start for another two months. My mother took me to work with her every day. The agency she worked for did not like it, but she had no choice but to take me with her. After all, she could not very well leave me home alone.

On her day job at the nursing home, she cleaned up after bedridden old people. Some of the people were my grandmother's age, but could neither eat nor clean themselves alone. My mother removed their bed pads and washed their underarms and legs, then fed them at lunchtime.

I spent the days in the lounge watching a soap opera while an old black lady taught me how to knit a scarf.

The night job was much better. The old lady was asleep when my mother got there and took over the shift from someone else. My mother would go into the living room and open a cot for me to sleep on. Most nights, she slept on the floor in the old lady's room in case something happened in the middle of the night.

One night near the end of the summer, I asked her to stay with me for a little while. I was tired of being alone and I was missing home.

"If the lady screams, we will hear it," I said.

"She can't scream," my mother said. "She had a stroke and she can't speak."

She made some tea and stayed with me for a while, anyway.

"I don't sleep very much at night," she said. "Otherwise this would be very hard work to do."

I felt so sorry for her. She looked very sad. Her face was cloudy with fatigue even though she kept reapplying the cream she had bought to lighten her skin.

She laid out a comforter on the floor and stretched her body across it.

"I want you to know that this will change soon when I find a job that pays both for our expenses and for my mother's and Atie's."

"I wish I could help you do one of your jobs," I said.

"But I want you to go to school. I want you to get a doctorate, or even higher than that."

"I am sorry you work so hard," I said. "I never realized you did so much."

"That's how it is. Life is no vacation. If you get your education, there are things you won't have to do."

She turned over on her back and stared directly into my face, something she did not do very often.

It had been a month since I had seen Marc. I wondered if

he had gone away, but I didn't want to ask her in case he had and in case it was because of me.

"Am I the mother you imagined?" she asked, with her eyes half-closed.

As a child, the mother I had imagined for myself was like Erzulie, the lavish Virgin Mother. She was the healer of all women and the desire of all men. She had gorgeous dresses in satin, silk, and lace, necklaces, pendants, earrings, bracelets, anklets, and lots and lots of French perfume. She never had to work for anything because the rainbow and the stars did her work for her. Even though she was far away, she was always with me. I could always count on her, like one counts on the sun coming out at dawn.

"Was I the mother you imagined? You don't have to answer me," she said. "After you've seen me, I know the answer."

"For now I couldn't ask for better," I said.

"What do you think of Marc?" she asked, quickly changing the subject.

"I think he is smart."

"He helped me a lot in getting you here," she said, "even though he did not like the way I went about it. In Haiti, it would not be possible for someone like Marc to love someone like me. He is from a very upstanding family. His grandfather was a French man."

She began the story of how she met him. She talked without stopping, as though she were talking on one of our cassettes.

She got her green card through an amnesty program. When she was going through her amnesty proceedings, she had to get a lawyer. She found him listed in a Haitian newspaper and called his office. She was extremely worried that she would not be eligible for the program. It took him a long time to convince her that this was not the case and, over that period of time, they became friends. He started taking her to restaurants, always Haitian restaurants, sometimes ones as far away as Philadelphia. They even went to Canada once to eat at a Haitian restaurant in Montreal. Marc was old-fashioned about a lot of things and had some of the old ways. He had never married and didn't have any children back home—that he knew of—and she admired that. She was going to stay with him as long as he didn't make any demands that she couldn't fulfill.

"Are you going to marry?" I asked.

"*Jesus Marie Joseph*, I don't know," she said. "He is the first man I have been with in a long time."

She asked if there was a boy in Haiti that I had liked.

I said no and she smiled.

"You need to concentrate when school starts, you have to give that all your attention. You're a good girl, aren't you?"

By that she meant if I had ever been touched, if I had ever held hands, or kissed a boy.

"Yes," I said. "I have been good."

"You understand my right to ask as your mother, don't you?"

I nodded.

"When I was a girl, my mother used to test us to see if we were virgins. She would put her finger in our very private parts and see if it would go inside. Your Tante Atie hated it. She used to scream like a pig in a slaughterhouse. The way my mother was raised, a mother is supposed to do that to her daughter until the daughter is married. It is her responsibility to keep her pure."

She rubbed her palm against her eyelids, as if to keep the sleep away.

"My mother stopped testing me early," she said. "Do you know why?"

I said no.

"Did Atie tell you how you were born?"

From the sadness in her voice, I knew that her story was sadder than the chunk of the sky and flower petals story that Tante Atie liked to tell.

"The details are too much," she said. "But it happened like this. A man grabbed me from the side of the road, pulled me into a cane field, and put you in my body. I was still a young girl then, just barely older than you."

I did not press to find out more. Part of me did not understand. Most of me did not want to.

"I thought Atie would have told you. I did not know this man. I never saw his face. He had it covered when he did this to me. But now when I look at your face I think it is true what they say. A child out of wedlock always looks like its father."

She did not sound hurt or angry, just like someone who was stating a fact. Like naming a color or calling a name. Something that already existed and could not be changed. It took me twelve years to piece together my mother's entire story. By then, it was already too late.

Two

⋀⋀⋀⋀⋀⋀

Chapter 9

∧∨∧∨∧∨∧∨∧∨∧

I was eighteen and going to start college in the fall. My mother continued working her two jobs, but she put in even longer hours. And we moved to a one-family house in a tree-lined neighborhood near where Marc lived.

In the new place, my mother had a patch of land in the back where she started growing hibiscus. Daffodils would need more care and she had grown tired of them.

We decorated our new living room in red, everything from the carpet to the plastic roses on the coffee table. I had my very own large bedroom with a new squeaky bed. My mother's room was even bigger, with a closet that you could have entertained some friends in. In some places in Haiti, her closet would have been a room on its own, and the clothes would not have bothered the fortunate child who would sleep in it.

Before the move, I had been going to a Haitian Adventist

school that went from elementary right to high school. They had guaranteed my mother that they would get me into college and they had lived up to their pledge. Now my first classes at college were a few months away and my mother couldn't have been happier. Her sacrifices had paid off.

I never said this to my mother, but I hated the Maranatha Bilingual Institution. It was as if I had never left Haiti. All the lessons were in French, except for English composition and literature classes. Outside the school, we were "the Frenchies," cringing in our mock-Catholic-school uniforms as the students from the public school across the street called us "boat people" and "stinking Haitians."

When my mother was home, she made me read out loud from the English Composition textbooks. The first English words I read sounded like rocks falling in a stream. Then very slowly things began to take on some meaning. There were words that I heard often. Words that jump out of New York Creole conversations, like the last kernel in a cooling popcorn machine. Words, among others, like *TV, building, feeling,* which Marc and my mother used even when they were in the middle of a heated political discussion in Creole. *Mwin gin yon feeling. I have a feeling Haiti will get back on its feet one day, but I'll be dead before it happens.* My mother, always the pessimist.

There were other words that helped too, words that looked almost the same in French, but were pronounced differently in English: *nationality, alien, race, enemy, date, present.* These and other words gave me a context for the rest that I did not understand.

Eventually, I began to hear myself that I read better. I answered swiftly when my mother asked me a question in

English. Not that I ever had a chance to show it off at school, but I became an English speaker.

"There is great responsibility that comes with knowledge," my mother would say. My great responsibility was to study hard. I spent six years doing nothing but that. School, home, and prayer.

Tante Atie once said that love is like rain. It comes in a drizzle sometimes. Then it starts pouring and if you're not careful it will drown you.

I was eighteen and I fell in love. His name was Joseph and he was old. He was old like God is old to me, ever present and full of wisdom.

He looked somewhat like Monsieur Augustin. He was the color of ground coffee, with a cropped beard and a voice like molasses that turned to music when he held a saxophone to his lips.

He broke the monotony of my shuffle between home and school when he moved into the empty house next door to ours.

My mother never trusted him. In the back of my mind echoed her constant warning, "You keep away from those American boys." The ones whose eyes followed me on the street. The ones who were supposedly drooling over me afterwards, even though they called me a nasty West Indian to my face. "You keep away from them especially. They are upset because they cannot have you."

Aside from Marc, we knew no other men. Men were as mysterious to me as white people, who in Haiti we had only known as missionaries. I tried to imagine my mother's reaction to Joseph. I could already hear her: "Not if he were the last unmarried man on earth."

When she came home during the day and saw him sitting on his porch steps next door, she would nod a quick hello and walk faster. She wrapped her arms tighter around me, as though to rescue me from his stare.

Somehow, early on, I felt that he might like me. The way his eyes trailed me up the block gave him away. My mother liked to say, "I admire priests because they like women for more than their faces and their buttocks." Joseph's look went beyond the face and the buttocks.

He looked like the kind of man who could buy a girl a meal without asking for her bra in return.

Whenever I went by his stoop, I felt like we were conspiring. How could I smile without my mother noticing and how could he respond to her brisk hello and mine too, without letting her see that wink that was for me alone?

At night, I fantasized that he was sitting somewhere pining away, dreaming about me, thinking of a way to enter my life. Then one day, like rain, he came to my front door.

I was stretched out on the couch with a chemistry book when I heard the knock. I looked through the security peephole to check. It was him.

"Can I use your phone?" he asked. "I've had mine disconnected because I'm going out of town soon."

I opened the door and led him to the phone. Our fingers touched as I handed it to him. He dialed quickly, smiling with his eyes on my face.

"Did we get it?" he asked into the phone.

His feet bounced off the ground when he heard the answer. "Yes!" he shouted. "Yes!"

68

He handed me back the phone with a wink.

"Have you ever really wanted something great and gotten it?" he asked.

My face must have been blank.

He asked me the question again, then suddenly slapped his forehead.

"I haven't even introduced myself."

"My name is Sophie," I said, jumping ahead.

"I am Joseph," he said. I knew.

"Was it good news you just got?"

"What gave me away?"

He looked at me as though he was waiting for me to say something equally witty. I wasn't as glib, as fast on my feet. I couldn't think of anything.

"It *was* good news," he answered. "I just found out that we got a gig in the East Village from now until our tour starts."

"A gig?"

"A job. I am a musician."

"I know," I said. "Sometimes I hear you playing at night."

"Does it bother you?"

"*Non*, it's very pretty."

"I detect an accent," he said.

Oh please, say a small one, I thought. After seven years in this country, I was tired of having people detect my accent. I wanted to sound completely American, especially for him.

"Where are you from?" he asked.

"Haiti."

"Ah," he said, "I have never been there. Do you speak Creole?"

"*Oui, Oui*," I ventured, for a laugh.

69

"We, we," he said, pointing to me and him. "We have something in common. *Mwin aussi*. I speak a form of Creole, too. I am from Louisiana. My parents considered themselves what we call Creoles. Is it a small world or what?"

I shook my head yes. It was a very small world.

"You live alone?" he asked.

My mother's constant suspicion prodded me and I quickly said, "No." Just in case he was thinking of coming over tonight to kill me. This was New York, after all. You could not trust anybody.

"I live with my mother."

"I have seen her," he said.

"She works."

"Nights?"

"Sometimes."

"Did you two just move here?"

"Yes, we did."

"I thought so," he said. "Whenever I'm in New York, I sublet in the neighborhood and I have never seen you walking around before."

"We moved about a year ago."

"That's about the last time I was in Brooklyn."

"Where are you the rest of the year?"

"In Providence."

I was immediately fascinated by the name. Providence. Fate! A town named for the Creator, the Almighty. Who would not want to live there?

"I am away from my house about six months out of the year," he said. "I travel to different places with my band and then after a while I go back for some peace and quiet."

"What is it like in Providence?" I asked.

"It is calm. I can drive to the river and watch the sun set. I think you would like it there. You seem like a deep, thoughtful kind of person."

"I am."

"I like that in people. I like that very much."

He glanced down at his feet as though he couldn't think of anything else to say.

I wanted to ask him to stay, but my mother would be home soon.

"I work at home," he finally said, "in case you ever want to drop by."

I spent the whole week with my ear pressed against the wall, listening to him rehearse. He rehearsed day and night, sometimes twelve to ten hours without stopping. Sometimes at night, the saxophone was like a soothing lullaby.

One afternoon, he came by with a ham-and-cheese sandwich to thank me for letting him use the phone. He sat across from me in the living room while I ate very slowly.

"What are you going to study in college?" he asked.

"I think I am going to be a doctor."

"You think? Is this something you like?"

"I suppose so," I said.

"You have to have a passion for what you do."

"My mother says it's important for us to have a doctor in the family."

"What if you don't want to be a doctor?"

"There's a difference between what a person wants and what's good for them."

"You sound like you are quoting someone," he said.

"My mother."

"What would Sophie like to do?" he asked.

That was the problem. Sophie really wasn't sure. I had never really dared to dream on my own.

"You're not sure, are you?"

He even understood my silences.

"It is okay not to have your future on a map," he said. "That way you can flow wherever life takes you."

"That is not Haitian," I said. "That's very American."

"What is?"

"Being a wanderer. The very idea."

"I am not American," he said. "I am African-American."

"What is the difference?"

"The African. It means that you and I, we are already part of each other."

I think I blushed. At least I nearly choked on my sandwich. He walked over and tapped my back.

"Are you all right?"

"I am fine," I said, still short of breath.

"I think you are a fine woman," he said.

I started choking again.

I knew what my mother would think of my going over there during the day. A good girl would never be alone with a man, an older one at that. I wasn't thinking straight. It was nice waking up in the morning knowing I had someone to talk to.

I started going next door every day. The living room was bare except for a couch and a few boxes packed in a corner near his synthesizer and loud speakers.

At first I would sit on the linoleum and listen to him play. Then slowly, I moved closer until sometimes he would let me touch the keyboard, guiding my fingers with his hand on top of mine.

Between strokes, I learned the story of his life. He was from a middle-class New Orleans family. His parents died when he was young. He was on his own by the time he was fifteen. He went to college in Providence but by his sophomore year left school and bought a house there. He was lucky he had been left enough money to pursue his dream of being a musician. He liked to play slave songs, Negro spirituals, both on his saxophone and his piano, slowing them down or speeding them up at different tempos. One day, he would move back to Providence for good, and write his own songs.

I told him about Croix-des-Rosets, the Augustins, and Tante Atie. They would make a great song, he said. He had been to Jamaica, Cuba, and Brazil several times, trying to find links between the Negro spirituals and Latin and island music.

We went to a Haitian record store on Nostrand Avenue. He bought a few albums and we ate lunch every day listening to the drum and conch shell beats.

"I am going to marry you," he said at lunch one day. "Even though I already know the problems that will arise. Your mother will pass a watermelon over it, because I am so old."

Ever since we had become friends, I'd stopped thinking of

him as old. He talked young and acted young. As far as I was concerned he could have been my age, but with more nurtured kindness, as Tante Atie liked to say.

"You are not very old," I told him.

"Not very old, huh?"

"Age doesn't matter."

"Only the young can say that. I am not sure your mother will agree."

"We won't have to tell her."

"She can tell I'm old just by looking at me."

"How old are you?"

"Old. Older than you."

One day when I was in his house, I sneaked a peek at his driver's license and saw the year that he was born. He was my mother's age, maybe a month or two younger.

"They say men look distinguished when they get old," I said.

"Easy for you to say."

"I believe in the young at heart."

"That's a very mature thing to say."

It was always sad to leave him at night. I wanted to go to hear him play with his band, but I was afraid of what my mother would think.

He knocked on my door very late one night. My mother was away, working the whole night. I came out and found him sitting on the steps out front. He still had on his black tuxedo, which he had worn to work. He brought me some posters of the legends who were his idols: Charlie Bird Parker and Miles Davis.

"Sophie, you should have heard me tonight," he said. "I was so hot you could have fried a plantain on my face."

We both laughed loudly, drawing glares from people passing by.

"Can you go out to eat?" he asked. "Somewhere, anywhere. I'm so high from the way I played, don't let me down."

I called my mother at the old lady's house, on the pretense that I was wishing her a good night. Then we drove to the Café des Arts on Long Island, which was always open late, Joseph said.

I drank my first cappuccino with a drop of rum. We shared a tiny cup; he was worried about driving back and finding my mother at home, waiting for me. He told me to raise my head through the roof of his convertible, as we sped on the freeway, hurrying to make it home before sunrise. I felt like I was high enough to wash my hair in a cloud and have a star in my mouth.

"I am being irresponsible," he said. "Your mother will have me arrested. Thank God you are over eighteen."

He held my hand on the doorstep, swaying my pinky back and forth.

"You do wonders for my English," I said, hoping it wasn't too forward.

"You're such a beautiful woman," he said.

"You think I am a woman? You're the first person who has called me that."

"In that sad case, everyone else is blind."

I leaned my head on his shoulder as we watched the morning sky lighten.

"Can you tell I like you?" he asked.

"I can tell."

"Do you like me?"

"You will not respect me if I say yes," I said.

He threw his head back and laughed.

"Where do you get such notions?"

"How do I know you're not just saying these things so you can get what you want."

"What do you think I want?" he asked.

"What all men want."

"Which is?"

"I don't want to say it."

"You will have to say it," he said. "What is it? Life? Liberty? The pursuit of happiness?" He quickly let go of my hand. "I'm not about that. I am older than that. I am not going to say I am better than that because I am not a priest, but I'm not about that."

"Then what do you want with me?" I asked.

"The pursuit of happiness."

"Are you asking me to be with you?"

"Yes. No. It's not the way you think. Let's just go to sleep, solitaire, separately. Fare thee well. Good night."

He waited for me to go inside. I locked the door behind me. I heard him playing his keyboard as I lay awake in bed. The notes and scales were like raindrops, teardrops, torrents. I felt the music rise and surge, tightening every muscle in my body. Then I relaxed, letting it go, feeling a rush that I knew I wasn't supposed to feel.

Chapter 10

∧∧∧∧∧∧∧∧∧∧

My mother came home early the next night.

"We're going out," she said. "We have not done anything, the two of us, in too long."

A musty heat surrounded us as we stood on the platform waiting for a subway train to come.

Inside the train, there were listless faces, people clutching the straps, hanging on. In Haiti, there were only sugar cane railroads that ran from the sugar mill in Port-au-Prince to plantation towns all over the countryside. Sometimes on the way home, some kids and I would chase the train and try to yank sugar cane sticks from between the wired bars.

As the D train sped over the Brooklyn Bridge, its lights swaying on the water below, my mother kept her eyes on the river, her face beaming as if she was a guest on the moon.

"Ah, if *Manman* would agree to come to America, then Atie would see this," she said.

"Do you think you'll ever go back to Haiti?" I asked.

"I have to go back to make final arrangements for your grandmother's resting place. I want to see her before she dies, but I don't want to stay there for more than three or four days. I know that sounds bad, but that is the only way I can do it. There are ghosts there that I can't face, things that are still very painful for me."

I waited for the train to sink below the city so I could have her full attention.

"I am past eighteen now," I said. "Is it okay if I like someone?"

"Do you like someone?" she asked.

"I am asking, just in case I do."

"Do you?"

"Yes."

"Who is it?" she asked.

I was afraid to tell her right away.

"Nothing has happened yet," I said.

"I would hope not," she said. "Who is it?"

She waited for me to speak, but I wanted to hold on to my secret just a bit longer.

"Let me tell you a few things," she said. "You have to get yourself a man who will do something for you. He can't be a vagabond. I won't have it."

"He is not a vagabond."

"How do you know? Do you think he will walk up to you and say, 'Hi, I am a vagabond'?"

"I trust—"

"You are already lost," she said. "You tell me you trust him and I know you are already lost. What's his name?"

Henry was the first name I could think of.

"Henry what?"

I thought hard for a last name for my Henry.

"Henry *Je ne sais quoi*."

"Don't you dare play with me."

"I was just joking," I said. "I know his last name. It is Henry Napoleon."

"Of the Leogane Napoleons?" My mother closed her eyes as though there was a long family registry in her brain.

The Leogane Napoleons? Why had I chosen them? There were more illustrious Haitian families. I could see my mother's mind working very quickly. Were they rich? Poor? Black? Mulatto? Were they of peasant stock? Literate? Professionals?

"I want to meet him," she said.

"He is not here." I thought quickly. "He went back to Haiti after graduation."

"Is he coming back?"

"I don't know."

"I want to meet his parents. It's always proper for the parents to talk first. That way if there's been any indiscretion, we can have a family meeting and arrange things together. It's always good to know the parents."

"The parents are in Haiti with him."

"Are they ever coming back?"

"I don't know."

"Find out. I want to meet them when they get back."

I leaned over and kissed her cheek to show her that I appreciated her trying to be a good mother. I wanted to tell her that I loved her, but the words would not roll off my tongue.

I had to be more careful now that my mother knew I had a love interest. I cooked all her favorite meals and had them ready for her when she got home. I even used the mortar and pestle to crush onions and spices to add those special flavors she liked. I got A and Bs in chemistry and tried to hide my chagrin whenever Joseph was on a gig in another part of the country.

My mother waited very patiently for Henry Napoleon of the Leogane Napoleons to come back from Haiti. Every time she asked about him, she took advantage of the moment to give me some general advice.

"It is really hard for the new-generation girls," she began. "You will have to choose between the really old-fashioned Haitians and the new-generation Haitians. The old-fashioned ones are not exactly prize fruits. They make you cook plantains and rice and beans and never let you feed them lasagna. The problem with the new generation is that a lot of them have lost their sense of obligation to the family's honor. Rather than become doctors and engineers, they want to drive taxicabs to make quick cash."

My mother had somehow learned from someone at work that the Leogane Napoleons were a poor but hard-working clan. She said that in Haiti if your mother was a coal seller and you became a doctor, people would still look down on you knowing where you came from. But in America, they like success stories. The worse off you were, the higher your praise. Henry's mother had sold coal in Haiti, but now her son was going to be a doctor. Henry's was a success story.

. . .

Joseph was away for a month. He sent me postcards and letters from the road. Each day I rushed to the mailbox, making sure I got them before my mother did. I put his jazz-legend posters on my walls and stared at them day and night.

Whenever my mother was home, I would stay up all night just waiting for her to have a nightmare. Shortly after she fell asleep, I would hear her screaming for someone to leave her alone. I would run over and shake her as she thrashed about. Her reaction was always the same. When she saw my face, she looked even more frightened.

"*Jesus Marie Joseph.*" She would cover her eyes with her hands. "Sophie, you've saved my life."

Chapter 11

∧∧∧∧∧∧∧∧∧

His first night back home, I went to hear Joseph play. My mother was working. I took a chance. I put on a tight-fitting yellow dress that I had hidden under my mattress. Joseph wore a tuxedo with a tie and cumberbund made of African kente cloth.

"You look like you're all grown up," he said.

"A lot of time has gone by," I said.

"What's time to you and me?"

"Out of sight, out of mind."

"Not your sight and not my mind."

He always knew all the right things to say.

In the car, he told me about how all the towns looked alike after a while when he was traveling and how he kept thinking about me and feeling guilty about my mother, because he was wanting to steal me away from her.

The whole evening was like one daydream. I had never

imagined myself in a place like the Note. There was a large dance floor with pink and yellow lights twinkling from the ceiling. That night Joseph played the tenor saxophone. There was a whimpering sound to it, like a mourning cry.

After the show, we drove over the bridge, into dawn.

"I have to go away again," he said, on the steps of my house. "We have to play in Florida. I think you would love Florida."

He took a small silver ring from his pinky and slipped it onto mine. I felt my eyes close. I let in my first kiss.

I did not see him for a while. He was back from Florida but packing to return to Providence. We went for dinner at the Note. This time he wasn't playing. We sat at a table with the other customers. He asked me to marry him.

I didn't say no, but I didn't say yes. I wanted time to think. My mother would never allow it. She would go crazy.

"Let's have dreams on it," he said, "and if you never bring it up again, neither will I."

That night, I slept hugging my secret.

When my mother came home from work, we went on another ride on the train to watch the lights on the bridge. I wanted to tell her that I loved someone. Like maybe she loved Marc, or like she had loved before.

"*Manman*, Henry Napoleon is never coming back," I said.

"It's too bad," she said. "I hear from Maryse at work that he is in medical school in Mexico."

"Really?"

"You didn't know? I thought he was the one sending you these letters from all over the country."

She was quiet as the train raced over the bridge and back down to the tunnel.

"There are secrets you can't keep," she said. "Not from your mother anyway."

The next night, after seeing Joseph, I came home to find my mother sitting in the living room. She was sitting there rocking herself, holding a belt in her hand.

"I thought you were dead," she said when I walked in.

I tried to tell her that I had not done anything wrong, but it was three in the morning. I wished that I had not asked Joseph to let me go in alone. Perhaps if he had been there. Who knows?

"Where were you?" She tapped the belt against her palm, her lifelines becoming more and more red. She took my hand with surprised gentleness, and led me upstairs to my bedroom. There, she made me lie on my bed and she tested me.

I mouthed the words to the Virgin Mother's Prayer: Hail Mary . . . so full of grace. The Lord is with You . . . You are blessed among women . . . Holy Mary. Mother of God. Pray for us poor sinners.

In my mind, I tried to relive all the pleasant memories I remembered from my life. My special moments with Tante Atie and with Joseph and even with my mother.

As she tested me, to distract me, she told me, "The Marassas were two inseparable lovers. They were the same person, duplicated in two. They looked the same, talked the same, walked the same. When they laughed, they even laughed the same and when they cried, their tears were identical. When one went to the stream, the other rushed under the water to get a better look. When one looked in the mirror, the other walked behind the glass to mimic her. What vain lovers they were, those *Marassas*. Admiring one another for being so much alike, for being copies. When you love someone, you want him to be closer to you than your *Marassa*. Closer than your shadow. You want him to be your soul. The more you are alike, the easier this becomes. When you look in a stream, if you saw that man's face, wouldn't you think it was a water spirit? Wouldn't you scream? Wouldn't you think he was hiding under a sheet of water or behind a pane of glass to kill you? The love between a mother and daughter is deeper than the sea. You would leave me for an old man who you didn't know the year before. You and I we could be like *Marassas*. You are giving up a lifetime with me. Do you understand?

"There are secrets you cannot keep," my mother said after the test.

She pulled a sheet up over my body and walked out of the room with her face buried in her hands. I closed my legs and tried to see Tante Atie's face. I could understand why she had screamed while her mother had tested her. *There are secrets you cannot keep.*

Chapter 12

∧∧∧∧∧∧∧∧∧∧

I did not tell Joseph what happened. He left for Providence and stayed away for five weeks. My mother still worked night shifts. She had no choice. However, she would test me every week to make sure that I was still *whole*.

When Joseph returned, I did my best to avoid him. I was hoping he would go back to Providence and forget that he had ever met me. He did not give up so easily. One night he banged on the door for two hours and finally I opened it.

"I'm leaving for Providence after next week for good," he said coldly. "I wanted to know if there was anything in this house you wanted."

"I don't want anything," I said, walking away.

I twirled the ring around my fingers while listening to the saxophone wailing in the dark. My mother rarely spoke to me since she began the tests. When she went out with Marc, I refused to go and she showed no desire to take me along.

I was feeling alone and lost, like there was no longer any reason for me to live. I went down to the kitchen and searched my mother's cabinet for the mortar and pestle we used to crush spices. I took the pestle to bed with me and held it against my chest.

The story goes that there was once a woman who walked around with blood constantly spurting out of her unbroken skin. This went on for twelve long years. The woman went to many doctors and specialists, but no one could heal her. The blood kept gushing and spouting in bubbles out of her unbroken skin, sometimes from her arms, sometimes from her legs, sometimes from her face and chest. It became a common occurrence, soaking her clothes a bright red on very special occasions—weddings and funerals. Finally, the woman got tired and said she was going to see Erzulie to ask her what to do.

After her consultation with Erzulie, it became apparent to the bleeding woman what she would have to do. If she wanted to stop bleeding, she would have to give up her right to be a human being. She could choose what to be, a plant or an animal, but she could no longer be a woman.

The woman was tired of bleeding, so she went home and divided her goods among her friends and loved ones. Then she went back to Erzulie for her transformation.

"What form of life do you want to take?" asked Erzulie. "Do you want to be a green lush plant in a garden? Do you want to be a gentle animal in the sea? A ferocious beast of the night?"

The woman thought of all the animals that she had seen,

the ones that people feared and others that they loved. She thought of the ones that were small. Ones that were held captive and ones that were free.

"Make me a butterfly," she told Erzulie. "Make me a butterfly."

"A butterfly you shall be," said Erzulie.

The woman was transformed and never bled again.

My flesh ripped apart as I pressed the pestle into it. I could see the blood slowly dripping onto the bed sheet. I took the pestle and the bloody sheet and stuffed them into a bag. It was gone, the veil that always held my mother's finger back every time she tested me.

My body was quivering when my mother walked into my room to test me. My legs were limp when she drew them aside. I ached so hard I could hardly move. Finally I failed the test.

My mother grabbed me by the hand and pulled me off the bed. She was calm now, resigned to her anger.

"Go," she said with tears running down her face. She seized my books and clothes and threw them at me. "You just go to him and see what he can do for you."

I waited until I heard her moaning in her sleep. I gathered my things and stuffed them into a suitcase. I had to dress quickly. I tiptoed downstairs and opened the front door.

I knocked on Joseph's door and waited for him to answer.

"Are you in trouble?" he asked.

He took me inside and sat me down.

I was limping a little. My body ached from the wound the pestle had made. I handed him my suitcase and the pinky ring he had given me.

"I am ready for a real ring," I said.

"You want to get married?"

I nodded.

"But we have to do it now," I said. "Right this very minute."

"Without a priest?"

"I don't care."

I was bound to be happy in a place called Providence. A place that destiny was calling me to. Fate! A town named after the Creator, the Almighty. Who would not want to live there?

Three

⋀⋅⋀⋅⋀⋅⋀⋅⋀

Chapter 13

⋀⋁⋀⋁⋀⋁⋀⋁⋀⋁

"Great gods in Guinea, you are beautiful," the driver said as he stopped under a breadfruit tree in the middle of the sheds, stands, and clusters of women in the open marketplace.

I lowered my head and pretended not to hear, but he persisted.

"I would crawl inside your dress and live there. I can feed on your beauty like a leech feeds on blood. I would live and die for you. More than the sky loves its stars. More than the night loves its moon. More than the sea loves its mermaids. *Strike me, thunder, it's no lie.* We do not know one another, I know. Still I must tell you. You can be the core of my existence. The 'I' of my 'We.' The first and last letter of my name, which is 'Yours,' your humble servant and transporter."

It was a stifling August day. The sun, which was once god

to my ancestors, slapped my face as though I had done something wrong. The fragrance of crushed mint leaves and stagnant pee alternated in the breeze. Body-raking soka blared from the car radio as passengers hopped off the colorful van in which I had spent the last four hours.

The sides of the van were painted in steaming reds, from cherry scarlet to crimson blood. Giraffes and lions were sketched over a terra cotta landscape, as though seeking a tint of green.

I wouldn't have gotten the coveted seat next to the driver had it not been for what he termed my "young charcoal-cloaked beauty." Otherwise, I would have been forced to sit with the market women, their children, livestock, wicker baskets, and the flour sacks that shielded their backs from the sugar cane stalks.

DIEU SI BON proclaimed the letters on the van's front plate. God is good indeed. Otherwise, my daughter, Brigitte, and I would have never made it this far.

"A wonderful trip, *pa vrè?*" asked the driver, as he unloaded my suitcase.

"At least we arrived," I said.

"It is not my fault, lovely star, if we rocked a little. There are dunes and ridges on the road that I did not put there."

"I am not blaming you for those. On the contrary, I am very grateful we've arrived safely."

"All my trips have not been safe. You must be an angel. You bring good blessings. I have been in a ravine or two in the past."

"And your passengers?"

"I would hope they are in heaven."

94

He peeled a white T-shirt off his chest. Sweat rolled in dancing ripples from his neck to his belly. His skin was a bright chestnut, like mine and Brigitte's.

"You hot too?" he asked.

"It's dangerous for a woman to undress in public," I said.

"Still, I would love to see if you look like a goddess naked. Is there any way you can be persuaded?"

"Mwin, I am a married woman."

"I see that," he said, pointing first to my wedding ring and then to my daughter. "She is as perfect as you are, the child."

"Ou byen janti." You are very kind.

"I find your Creole flawless," he said.

"This is not my first trip to La Nouvelle Dame Marie. I was born here."

"I still commend you, my dear. People who have been away from Haiti fewer years than you, they return and pretend they speak no Creole."

"Perhaps they can't."

"Is it so easy to forget?"

"Some people need to forget."

"Obviously, you do not need to forget," he said.

"I need to remember."

An old hunchbacked lady walked over to pay her fare. He straightened out the dirty *gourdes* and counted them quickly.

She walked to the back of the van and pointed out her load of sorghum to a sweaty teenage boy. The boy had a *bourèt*, a handcart made out of two tires and a slab of plywood. He had a group of helpers, younger lads with dust-crusted feet. A young boy followed them with a kite. He ran ahead, tugging the kite string, trying to force it to fly above his head. The old woman nearly tripped over the kite as it crashed to the ground.

Brigitte stirred in my arms. She opened her eyes, fluttered her long eyelashes, and then closed them again. A mild breeze rustled the guava trees that now lined the unpaved road. The breeze swept the soil from the hills down to the valley, back to my grandmother's home.

Brigitte opened her mouth widely, stretching her lips to their limits as she yawned.

"I think Mademoiselle needs to eat again," the driver said.

He was looking across the road, at a woman sitting in a stand that was the size of a refrigerator. She was plump and beautiful with a bright russet complexion. She had a sky blue scarf wrapped around her head and two looped earrings bouncing off her cheeks.

It was Louise, Man Grace's daughter. At the window in front of her was a row of cola bottles.

"While you wait for your people, would you like something to drink?" asked the driver.

"I could drink an ocean," I said.

"If Mademoiselle over there is selling an ocean, I will surely buy it for you."

The female street vendors called to one another as they came down the road. When one merchant dropped her heavy basket, another called out of concern, "*Ou libéré?*" Are you free from your heavy load?

The woman with the load would answer yes, if she had unloaded her freight without hurting herself.

. . .

96

I sat in the shade of a crimson flamboyant tree, at the turn of the forked road. Brigitte quickly tightened her lips around the bottle of milk that I gave her. She sucked the warm liquid as though she hadn't been fed for days.

A few Tonton Macoutes climbed into the van and settled in the empty seats to eat their lunch. The steaming banana leaves and calabash bowls were in sharp contrast to their denim militia uniforms. They laughed loudly as they threw pieces of grilled meat and small biscuits at each other.

"I have a pig to sell you," whispered a voice behind me.

I was startled. My body plunged forward. I tightened my grip on Brigitte and nearly pushed the bottle down her throat. Brigitte began to cry, spitting the milk out of her mouth.

"Do you have all your senses?" I shouted at the woman.

Her face was hidden behind the flamboyant's drooping branches.

I raised Brigitte over my shoulder and tapped her back to burp her.

"Pardon. Pardon," Louise said, walking out from behind the tree. "I did not mean to scare you."

The driver was sitting at the stand, in her place, collecting coins and popping the caps off before handing foaming bottles to her customers.

I rocked Brigitte until she quieted down.

"I have a pig," Louise said, sitting on the rusty grass patch next to me.

The tree bark scraped my back as I tried to slide upright.

"Will you look at my pig?" she insisted. "I look at you, I see one who loves all God's creatures."

"I have no use for a pig," I said.

97

"It's a *piyay*, a steal, for five hundred *gourdes*."

"I don't need one." I said, shaking my head. "Please, have you seen my Tante Atie?"

"I know you. I do," she said.

"You know Atie too."

"For sure, I know Atie. We are like milk and coffee, lips and tongue. We are two fingers on the same hand. Two eyes on the same head."

"Do you know where she is? She was supposed to meet me here. I sent her a cassette from America."

"How is there?" Her eyes were glowing. "Is it like they say? Large? Grand? Are there really pennies on the streets and lots of maids' jobs? Mwin *rélé* Louise."

"I know who you are."

"My mother was Man Grace."

"I know," I said.

"Gone, my mother is dead now," she said. "She is in Guinea ahead of me. Now I know you too. You are Sophie. Atie can never make herself stop talking about you. I am teaching Atie her letters now and all she can write in her book is your name."

"I hope she will recognize me when she sees me."

"Folks like Atie know their people the moment they lay eyes on them."

"I have changed a lot since the baby. I bet she has changed too."

"Atie? That old maid, change?"

"You are friends, you say?"

"We are both alone in the world, since my mother died."

"What could be keeping Tante Atie," I wondered out loud.

"The wind will bring her soon. It will. Can I ask you a question?"

"What is it?"

"What do you do in America, Sophie? What is your profession?"

"I am *dactylo*," I said.

"*Ki sa?*"

"A secretary."

"You make money?"

"I haven't worked since I had the baby."

"Had enough for this journey, *non?*"

"I didn't plan on this journey."

I laid Brigitte on my lap. Her cheeks swayed back and forth like flesh balloons.

"I want to go to America," Louise said. "I am taking a boat."

"It is very dangerous by boat."

"I have heard everything. It has been a long time since our people walked to Africa, they say. The sea, it has no doors. They say the sharks from here to there, they can eat only Haitian flesh. That is all they know how to eat."

"Why would you want to make the trip if you've heard all that?"

"Spilled water is better than a broken jar. All I need is five hundred *gourdes*."

"I know the other side. Thousands of people wash up on the shores. They put it on television, in newspapers."

"People here too. We pray for them and bury them. Stop. Let us stop talking so sad. It is bad luck in front of a baby. How old is your baby?"

She reached over and tickled Brigitte's forehead.

"Twenty weeks."

"The birthing? What it feel like?"

"Like passing watermelons."

"*Wou.*" She cringed. "You look very mèg, bony. Not like women here who eat to fill a hole after their babies come out. When you were pregnant, you didn't eat corn so the baby could be yellow?"

"I never thought of that."

"You should have eaten honey so her hair would be soft."

"I will remember that."

"The next time, maybe?"

"Maybe."

"Your daughter? What is her name?"

"Brigitte Ifé Woods."

"Woods? It is not a Haitian name."

"No, non. Her father, he is American."

She called the boy with the kite over and squeezed a penny between his muddy fingers. With a few whispers in the child's ear, she sent him dashing down the road.

She rushed across to her stand and came back with a bottle of papaya cola.

My whole body felt cooler as the liquid slipped down my throat.

"I know you will pay me later," she said.

Tante Atie was standing at the crossroads, with a very wide grin on her pudgy face. She had not changed at all. She walked with her hands supporting her back, as if it hurt her. A panama hat tightly covered her head. On her shoulder was a palmetto sewing basket, flapping against her wide buttocks.

"She must have been on the way," Louise said.

"*Mim mwoin!*" I shouted to Tante Atie. I'm over here!

Tante Atie raced towards us. She had to look at me closely to see the girl she had put on the plane. It seemed so very long ago. The years had changed me.

"You are already chewing off my niece's ear," she said, tapping Louise's behind. "Always trying to give away your soul."

Louise sprang back to her stand.

"I would throw myself around you," my aunt said. "I would, just like a blanket, but I don't want to flatten the baby."

I handed Brigitte to her, as I raised myself from the ground.

"Who would have imagined it?" she said. "The precious one has your *manman*'s black face. She looks more like Martine's child than yours."

Chapter 14

⋀⋁⋀⋁⋀⋁⋀⋁⋀⋁⋀

Leaves were still piling up on the creeks along the road. A tall girl passed us with a calabash balancing on her head.

I carried a small suitcase, mostly filled with Brigitte's things. Brigitte napped as Tante Atie carried her in her arms.

The women we met on the road called Tante Atie *Madame*, even though she had never married.

"I cannot see this child coming out of you," Tante Atie said, rocking Brigitte in her arms.

"Sometimes, I cannot see it myself."

"Makes me think back to when you were this small and I had you in my arms. Feels the same too. Like I am holding something very valuable. Do you sometimes think she is going to break in your hands?"

"She is a true Caco woman; she is very strong."

A woman was sitting by the road stringing factory sequins together, while her daughter braided her hair.

"Louise tells me you've learned your letters," I said to Tante Atie.

"She must think I want that shouted from the hills."

"I was very happy to hear it."

"I alway felt, I did, that I knew words in my head. I did not know them on paper. Now once every so often, I put some nice words down. Louise, she calls them poems."

An old lady was trying to kill a rooster in the yard behind her house. The rooster escaped her grasp and ran around headless until it collapsed in the middle of the road. We walked around the bloody trail as the lady picked up the dead animal.

"Have you brought your daughter to Martine?" Tante Atie asked.

"She never answers my letters. When I called her, she slammed the phone down on me. She has not seen my daughter. We have not spoken since I left home."

"That's very sad for both of you. Very sad since you and Martine don't have anybody else over there. And Martine's head is not in the best condition."

A man hammered nails into a coffin in front of his roadside hut.

"*Honneur*, Monsié Frank," Tante Atie called out to the coffin builder.

"Respect." He flashed back a friendly smile.

"We have always heard that it is grand there," said Tante Atie. "Is it really as grand as they say, New York?"

"It's a place where you can lose yourself easily."

"Grand or not grand, I am losing myself here too."

We passed Man Grace's farm, with the bamboo fence around it. The house was worn out and wind-whipped. There were large wooden boards on the windows.

"When did Man Grace die?" I asked Tante Atie.

"Almost the day I came back to live here," she said.

"What was wrong with her?"

"She went to bed and just stopped breathing. It must have been her time. It was very hard on Louise when her manman died. Louise and Grace, they had slept in the same bed all her life. Louise was in the bed when Grace went to Guinea. To this day, it tears her open to sleep alone."

My grandmother's house still looked the same. I dropped my suitcase on the porch and followed Tante Atie out to the back.

Grandmè Ifé was sprinkling water in the dust, before doing her sweeping.

"Old woman, I brought your children," Tante Atie said.

"Age and wedlock tames the beast," said my grandmother. "Am I looking at Sophie?"

I moved closer, pressing her fingers against my cheeks.

"Did you even have breasts the last time I saw you?" asked my grandmother.

"It has not been that long," Tante Atie said.

My grandmother's eyes were filled with tears. She buried her face in my chest and wrapped her arms around my waist.

"I called my daughter Brigitte Ifé," I said. "The Ifé is after you."

She stretched her neck to get a closer look.

"Do you see my granddaughter?" she asked, tracing her thumb across Brigitte's chin. "The tree has not split one mite. Isn't it a miracle that we can visit with all our kin, simply by looking into this face?"

Chapter 15

∧∧∧∧∧∧∧∧∧∧

The lights on a distant hill glowed like a candle light vigil. We ate supper at the small table on the back porch.

A New York skyline was emblazoned in sequins across Tante Atie's chest. I had hurriedly bought a matching pair of I LOVE NEW YORK sweatshirts for her and my grandmother, forgetting about the lifelong *deuil*, which kept my grandmother from wearing anything but black, to mourn my grandfather.

My grandmother chewed endlessly on the same piece of meat, as her eyes travelled back and forth between my face and Tante Atie's chest. I swallowed a mouthful of soursop juice, savoring the heavy screen of brown sugar lingering on my tongue.

"Does your mother still cook Haitian?" asked Tante Atie with a full mouth.

"I am not sure," I said.

My grandmother lowered her eyelids, sheltered her displeasure, and continued chewing.

"And you? Can you make some dishes?" Tante Atie asked.

"You will have to let me cook a meal," I said.

A small draft blew the cooking embers through the yard. My daughter eagerly clawed my neck as I slipped her bottle into her mouth.

"Do you go there again tonight?" my grandmother asked Tante Atie.

"The reading, it takes a lot of time," Tante Atie said.

"Why do you not go to the reading classes?"

"You want me to go the whole distance at night?"

"If you had your lessons elsewhere," said my grandmother, "they would be during the day. The way you go about free in the night, one would think you a devil."

"The night is already in my face, it is. Why should I be afraid of it?"

"I would like it better if you were learning elsewhere."

"I like where I am."

"Can you read only by moonlight?"

"Knowledge, you do not catch it in the air, old woman. I have to labor at it. Is that not right, Sophie?"

My grandmother did not give me a chance to answer.

"You can only labor in the night?"

"Reading, it is not like the gifts you have. I was not born with it."

"Most people are born with what they need," said my grandmother.

"I was born short of my share."

"You say that to your Makers when you see them in Guinea."

"Do not send me off to my Makers, old woman. Besides, my Makers should hear me from this place." My aunt raised her head to the star-filled sky. "Hear me! Great gods that made the moon and the stars. You see what you have done to me. You were stingy with the clay when you made this creature."

"Blasphemy!" spat my grandmother. "Why can't the girl come here and teach you your letters?"

Tante Atie got up from the table and walked to the yard. She poured some juice over the cooking ashes as she came back to collect our plates.

She took the plates to the yard, scrubbed them with a soap-soaked palm leaf, then laid them out to dry.

"Before you go into the night, why don't you read to us from your reading book?"

My grandmother shut both her eyes as she twirled a rooster feather in her ear.

Tante Atie walked into the house and came back with a composition notebook wrapped in brown paper. She raised the notebook so it covered her face and slowly began to read. At first she stuttered but soon her voice took on an even flow.

She read the very same words as those I'd written on the card that I had made for her so long ago, on Mother's Day.

> My mother is a daffodil,
> limber and strong as one.
> My mother is a daffodil,
> but in the wind, iron strong.

When she was done, she raised her head from behind the pages and snapped the notebook shut.

"I have never forgotten those words. I have written them down."

She got up and began walking away. "I am off into the night," she said. "The spirits of alone-ness, they call to me."

They put me in my mother's room. It had the same four-poster bed and the same mahogany wardrobe with giant hibiscus carved all over it. The mirror on the wardrobe had a wide reflection so that you could see what was happening out on the front and back porches. Even as far as the *tcha tcha* tree out towards the road.

The mattress sank as I sat on the bed, changing my daughter by the light of a *tèt gridap*, a tin-can lamp, named after bald-headed girls.

My grandmother was sleeping in the next room. She mumbled in her sleep, like an old warrior in the midst of a battle. My mother used to make the same kinds of sounds. *Lagé mwin.* Leave me alone.

I lay on the mattress with my daughter on my belly. Her breath felt soothing and warm against my bare skin. All we were missing was Joseph.

When I was pregnant, Joseph would play his saxophone for us, alone in the dark. He would put the horn very close to my stomach and blow in a soft whisper. Brigitte would come alive inside me, tickling like a feather under my skin. Joseph would press his ear against my stomach to hear her every move. He was always afraid that her sudden rotations would hurt me inside. We would both get real quiet, to give her a chance to calm down. Sometimes if she had trouble going to sleep, he would stroke my belly and both she and I would doze off immediately.

I put on one of Joseph's old shirts to sleep in. Tracing my fingers across my daughter's spine, I asked her questions that she could not possibly answer, questions that even I didn't know the answers to.

"Are you going to remember all of this? Will you be mad at Mommy for severing you from your daddy? Are you going to inherit some of Mommy's problems?"

My daughter was shaking slightly beneath her night shirt. I felt a sudden urge to tell her a story. When I was a little girl, Tante Atie had always seen to it that I heard a story, especially when I could not sleep at night.

"Crick."

"Crack?"

"Honor?"

"Respect."

There was magic in the images that she had made out of the night. She would rock my body on her lap as she told me of fishermen and mermaids bravely falling in love. The mermaids would leave stars for the fishermen to pick out of the sand. For the most beloved fishermen, the mermaids would leave their combs, which would turn to gold when the fishermen kissed them.

Brigitte woke up with a loud wail. She moaned, reaching up to touch my face. I picked up a wet towel and rubbed it over her body.

After her feeding, I opened the window a crack. My grandmother would scold me if she knew I was letting the night air into the house.

Tante Atie was standing in the yard, waving to an invisible

face. I walked away from the window and lay back down on the bed with my daughter.

My grandmother was pacing loudly in the next room as Tante Atie giggled loudly in the yard. It sounded like she had been drinking. Tante Atie walked up to the house, her feet pounding the cement.

"Is the lesson over?" asked my grandmother.

"Old woman, you will wake up Sophie," Tante Atie said.

"White hair is a crown of glory," said my grandmother.

"I don't have white hair," said Tante Atie.

"Only good deeds demand respect. Do you not want Sophie to respect you?"

"Sophie is not a child anymore, old woman. I do not have to be a saint for her."

Chapter 16

∧∧∧∧∧∧∧∧∧

I got up to watch the sun rise. I sat on the back steps, as clouds of smoke rose from charcoal pits all over the valley. A few small lizards darted through the dew-laden grass, their gizzards bloated like bubble gum. A group of women came trotting along the road, sitting side-saddle on overloaded mules.

I walked into a small wooden shack, split by a wall of tin into a latrine and a bathing room. In the bathing room was a metal basin filled with leaves and rainwater.

Even though so much time had passed since I'd given birth, I still felt extremely fat. I peeled off Joseph's shirt and scrubbed my flesh with the leaves in the water. The stems left tiny marks on my skin, which reminded me of the giant goose bumps my mother's testing used to leave on my flesh.

I raised a handful of leaves to my nose. They were a potpourri of flesh healers: catnip, senna, sarsaparillas, corrosol, the petals of blood red hibiscus, forget-me-nots, and daffodils.

After the bath, I wrapped a towel around me and ran back inside the house. My grandmother was sitting on the edge of her canopy bed. Her mattress had open seams where she stuffed her most precious belongings.

"Sophie, sé ou?"

"It's me." I said, standing in the doorway.

Her room was crowded with old baskets, dusty crates, and rusting steel drums. On an old dresser was a statue of Erzulie, our goddess of love who doubled for us as the Virgin Mother. Her face was the color of corn, and wrapped around her long black hair was a tiny blue handkerchief.

I went to Tante Atie's room to get Brigitte. Tante Atie was bouncing up and down on her four-poster bed with Brigitte between her legs. Her room had no windows. Instead, she had large quilts with bird and fish patterns, over the louvers on her wall.

I took Brigitte back to my room for a sponge bath. She giggled as I sprinkled scented talc between her legs. Her body was a bit warmer than usual. I looked for the infant thermometer that I had brought with me. I found it, broken in its case, the mercury scattered in the container.

There was splash in the bath house outside the window. My grandmother was naked in the bath shack, with the rickety door wide open. She raised a handful of leaves towards the four corners of the sky, then rapped the stems under her armpits. She swayed her body several times, shaking the leaves loose from her buttocks.

My grandmother had a curved spine and a pineapple-sized hump, which did not show through her clothes. Some years earlier, my mother had grown egg-sized mounds in both her breasts, then had them taken out of her.

Chapter 17

∧∧∧∧∧∧∧∧∧∧

We ate cassava sandwiches for breakfast. I dunked mine in a ceramic cup, steaming with dense black coffee. The cassava melted in the coffee, making one thick brew.

When I was younger, Tante Atie would always pass me more cassava once I had completely drowned my own.

Both Tante Atie and my grandmother ate their cassava properly. They chipped off the fragile ends with their teeth and then ventured a sip of the scalding coffee.

I kept my daughter on my lap as I dunked a spoon in the cup, trying to rescue the cassava. My grandmother glanced over at Tante Atie, then quickly looked away.

Tante Atie kept her head down as she ate. In the distance, a bell tolled from the cathedral in the town, the bell that early in the morning signaled indigents' funerals.

. . .

I abandoned the cassava and ran a small brush through Brigitte's hair, placing a small white barrette at the tip of a pigtail in the middle of her head.

My grandmother threw her head back and swallowed her coffee in one gulp. She reached into her blouse, pulled out a cracked clay pipe, and slipped the mouthpiece between her lips.

"I'm going to do the *maché*," announced my grandmother. She unhooked her satchel from the back of her chair as she got up from the table. One of her legs dragged slightly behind the other. The inside of her lagging foot was so callused that it had the same texture as the red dust in the yard.

"Can I come too?" I asked my grandmother.

"Surely," she said. "You just follow my shadow."

Brigitte let out a loud cry as I handed her to Tante Atie.

"Mommy will bring you a nice treat from the market," I said, hearing Tante Atie's voice echo from my childhood.

Brigitte shrieked loudly, her face tied up in tear-soaked knots.

"Hurry, go," urged Tante Atie.

I rushed down the road to catch up with my grandmother.

In the cane fields, the men were singing songs, once bellowed at the old *konbits*.

"*Bonjou,* Grandmè Ifé," they chanted.

"*Bonjou,* good men," replied my grandmother.

"This here is my granddaughter, Uncle Bazie," my grandmother said to an old man sitting on the side of the road.

He was slashing a machete across a thin piece of sugar cane. He took off his hat and bowed in my direction.

"Whereabouts she from?" asked the old man.

"Here," answered my grandmother. "She's from right here."

My grandmother shopped like an army general on rounds.

"Man Legros. Time is God's to waste, not ours. I want a few cinnamon barks, some ginger roots, and sweet potatoes to boil in my milk. Make the potatoes sweet enough so I won't need to put sugar in the milk."

"Only the Grand Master, He can do that," answered Man Legros, as she tugged at an old apron around her waist.

"I want me a *mamit* of red beans too," said my grand-mother. "The beans don't need sweetness."

She watched closely as Man Legros dug a tin cup into a hill of beans, spread out on a piece of cardboard on the ground.

"Give those beans some time to settle in the cup," said my grandmother. "Let them rest in the cup. Between you, between me. We know half of them is pebbles."

"No pebbles here," said Man Legros. She had a blackened silver tooth on either side of her mouth.

My grandmother reached inside her blouse and pulled out a small bundle. She unwrapped a cord around the little pouch, fished out a handful of crumpled *gourdes* and paid Man Legros.

Louise was sitting at her stand, selling colas to a few *Macoutes* dressed in bright denim uniforms and dark sun-glasses. They were the same ones who had gotten in the van yesterday. Louise was chatting and laughing along with them, as though they were all old friends.

One of them was staring at me. He was younger than the others, maybe even a teenager. He stood on the tip of his boots and shoved an old man aside to get a better look. I walked faster. He grabbed his crotch with one hand, blew me a kiss, then turned back to the others.

The kite boy was tugging at the young *Macoute's* starched denim pants, begging for a penny. The *Macoute* reached inside his pocket and handed the child a coin. The boy dashed across the road to buy a piece of sugar cane and mint candy.

My grandmother grabbed my hand and pulled me away. We walked up to a line of cloth and hat vendors with samples draped across their chests, and hats piled on their heads.

"I have this at home," said my grandmother, rubbing the edge of a white fabric against her face. "It will be for my burial."

"Have you come to buy my pig?" Louise asked. She followed us as we toured the fruit stands. My grandmother refused the mango chunks that the vendors handed to her, preferring instead to squeeze and pump the custard apples she wanted to buy.

"You well, Grandmè Ifé?" Louise asked, jumping in front of my grandmother.

"Oui, I got up this morning. I am well."

"And you Sophie, you well?"

"Very well," I answered. "Thank you."

"Will you buy the pig?"

"Don't you have things to look after?" snapped my grandmother.

The boy with the kite was sitting in Louise's stand for her. Louise kept following us, ignoring my grandmother's coldness.

"My foot, you see, you stepped on it!" The baby-faced *Macoute* was shouting at a coal vendor.

He rammed the back of his machine gun into the coal vendor's ribs.

"I already know the end," said my grandmother. She grabbed my hand and pulled me away. She wobbled quickly, her sandals hissing as the lazy foot swept across the ground.

Louise rushed back to her stand. My grandmother and I hurried to the *flamboyant* and started on the road home.

I turned back for one last look. The coal vendor was curled in a fetal position on the ground. He was spitting blood. The other *Macoutes* joined in, pounding their boots on the coal seller's head. Every one watched in shocked silence, but no one said anything.

My grandmother came back for me. She grabbed my hand so hard my fingers hurt.

"You want to live your nightmares too?" she hollered.

We walked in silence until we could hear the *konbit* song from the cane fields. The men were singing about a *platon-nade*, a loose woman who made love to the men she met by a stream and then drowned them in the water.

My grandmother spat in the dirt as we walked by Louise's shack.

"Are you mad at Louise?" I asked.

"People have died for saying the wrong things," answered my grandmother.

"You don't like Louise?"

"I don't like the way your Tante Atie has been since she came back from Croix-des-Rosets. Ever since she has come back, she and I, we are like milk and lemon, oil and water.

She grieves; she drinks *tafia*. I would not be surprised if she started wearing black for her father again."

"Maybe she misses Croix-des-Rosets."

"Better she go back, then. You bring a mule to water, but you cannot force it to drink the water. Why did she come back? If she had married there, would she not have stayed?"

"If she had married there, then you would be living with her and her husband."

"Those are the old ways," she said. "These days, they go so far, the children. People like me, we look after ourselves."

"Tante Atie wants to look after you."

"I looked after myself all the years she was in Croix-des-Rosets. I look after myself now. Next when we hear from your mother, I will ask her to send for Atie, so Atie can go and see New York, see the grandness like you have."

"Don't you want to go?"

"I have one foot in this world and one foot in the grave. Non, I do not want to go. But Atie, she should go. She cannot stay out of duty. The things one does, one should do out of love."

"Do you tell her that you do not want her to stay?"

"I would tell her if she ever engaged me in talk. Your Tante Atie she has changed a lot since she was with you. The reading, it is only one thing."

"I think it is very good that she has learned to read," I said. "It is her own freedom."

"There is a story that is told all the time in the valley. An old woman has three children. One dies in her body when she is pregnant. One goes to a faraway land to make her fortune and never does that one get to come back alive. The last one, she stays in the valley and looks after her mother."

Tante Atie was the last.

Chapter 18

∧∨∧∨∧∨∧∨∧∨∧∨

Tante Atie was stretched out in an old rocker. Brigitte lay on her lap. My grandmother took her beans to the yard to pick out the pebbles. She fanned a small fire with her hat, washed the beans, then put them to boil in a pot.

Brigitte yawned in her sleep as I picked her up. Tante Atie got up, grabbed her notebook from the floor, and peered at the pages. She held the notebook so close to her face, I thought there was a mirror inside.

"I did not realize you would remember the words of my card this long," I said.

"When you have something precious, you do not forget it."

She pressed her notebook against her chest as she started for the road.

"Are you going to the *maché?*" my grandmother called out.

"You need something?" asked Tante Atie.

"The *Macoutes* were doing damage," my grandmother said.

"Fighting?" asked Tante Atie.

"You just wait awhile," said my grandmother. "Don't go there now."

"Fighting who?" Tante Atie looked worried.

"I did not ask," said my grandmother.

"They hurt anybody?"

"The coal man, Dessalines."

"Dessalines? Why?"

"When people hate you they beat your animals. I don't know."

"Old woman, I am going to get a remedy for a lump in my calf and it cannot wait." Tante walked down the road, racing towards the marketplace.

"You have a lump on your calf?" asked my grandmother.

By then, Tante Atie was already gone.

My grandmother and I spent the day watching the beans boil. The kite boy wandered into the yard with a slingshot. He aimed his pebbles at a few small birds lodged in the *tcha tcha* tree. He had no successes, but kept trying, encouraged by an occasional cheer from my grandmother and me.

"Eliab, come get some water," my grandmother called out.

Eliab crawled under the porch where my mother kept a clay jug full of water. He soaked his stomach as he raised the jug to his lips.

. . .

The beans were cooked as the sun set. My grandmother mixed them with some maize, which we ate with chunks of avocado.

Tante Atie did not come home for supper. My grandmother put some food aside for her and left the rest in the pot.

I bathed Brigitte in a large pan that my grandmother dug out from under her bed, then gave her some formula before sitting down for supper. I felt both fat and guilty after eating my supper.

Eliab and two other boys crawled under the porch for some tin plates and spooned out their portions of the meal. They sat in a circle and ate quietly, like a clan of midget chiefs.

Brigitte tried to bring her left foot to her mouth, in order to suck her toes.

"She's a quiet child," my grandmother said.

"She's been like that since she was born."

"Crabs don't make papayas. Your mother, she was a quiet child too."

Brigitte reached over to grab my grandmother's nose.

"Your husband?" asked my grandmother, "Why did you leave him so suddenly?"

"I did not leave him for good," I said. "This is just a short vacation."

"Are you having trouble with any marital duties?"

"Yes," I answered honestly.

"What is it?"

"They say it is most important to a man."

"The night?"

"Oui."

"You cannot perform?" she asked. "You have trouble with the night? There must be some fulfillment. You have the child."

"It is very painful for me," I said.

She pulled her pouch from her pocket, pinched a few dabs of tobacco and stuffed them in her nostrils.

"Secrets remain secret only if we keep our silence," she said. "Your husband? Is he a good man?"

"He is a very good man, but I have no desire. I feel like it is an evil thing to do."

"Your mother? Did she ever test you?"

"You can call it that."

"That is what we have always called it."

"I call it humiliation," I said. "I hate my body. I am ashamed to show it to anybody, including my husband. Sometimes I feel like I should be off somewhere by myself. That is why I am here."

"Crick?" called my grandmother.

"Crack," answered the boys.

Their voices rang like a chorus, aiding my grandmother's entry into her tale.

"Tim, tim," she called.

"Bwa chèch," they answered. "Tale master, tell us your tale."

"The tale is not a tale unless I tell. Let the words bring wings to our feet."

"How many do you bring us tonight?"

"Tonight, only one story."

The night grew silent under her commanding tone. I lay on the bed with Brigitte, the open window allowing us a clear view of the sky. The stars fell as though the glue that held them together had come loose. They were not the stars you could wish upon. In Dame Marie, each time a star fell out of the sky, it meant that somebody would die.

"The story goes," said my grandmother, "that a lark saw a little girl, who he thought was the most beautiful little girl he had ever seen, from the top of his pomegranate tree."

She clapped her hands to the rhythm of the words.

"Now the lark, he wanted more than anything to have the little girl. So one day she was on the road, going to school. The lark stopped her and said to her, How would you like a nice sweet pomegranate, you pretty little girl? When she looked up at the tree, the girl was charmed by the lark. So handsome it was, with its red and green wings and long purple tail. It was a sight. And the pomegranate, it was a beauty too. Big as your head, it was. The girl thought she could eat for weeks and not be done eating that pomegranate, so she told the bird, Yes, I would like to have that pomegranate. The bird, it said, I will give it to you for the honor of just looking at your face.

"Every day it went like this. The girl got a pomegranate and the bird, it looked at her face. One day, the bird, it said, I will give you two pomegranates if only you would kiss me. The girl thought of how sweet the pomegranates were and how everyone was nice to her at school for her sharing the fruit with them, so that one day she kissed the bird and from then on always got two pomegranates.

"This went on for a while until one day the bird, it said, Would you like to go to a faraway land with me? You are so sweet and lovely. I would like to take you to a faraway land. The girl, she said, I don't know if I want to go away. The bird, it says, We will go by sea. The girl was afraid. She said, I do not want to leave my family, my village. The girl, she says, It is wet in the sea. You can go on my back—that is what the bird says. The girl, she said, I will not go. The bird, it got mad. It said, I am good enough to talk to. I am good enough to kiss. You eat my pomegranates, yet you will not go with me across the sea. The bird looked so sad, it looked like it was going to die of sadness. So the girl, she gave in to the bird and let him have his way. She said, I will go.

"As soon as the little girl got on the bird's back, the bird said to the girl, I didn't tell you this because it was a small thing, but in the land I am taking you to, there is a king there who will die if he does not have a little girl's heart. The girl she said, I didn't tell you this because it was a small thing, but little girls, they leave their hearts at home when they walk outside. Hearts are so precious. They don't want to lose them. The bird, clever as it was, it said to the girl, You might want to return to your home and pick up your heart. It is a small matter, but you may need it. So the girl, she said, Okay, let us go back and get my heart. The bird took her home and put her down on the ground. He told her he would wait for her to come back with her heart. The girl ran and ran all the way to her family village and never did she come back to the bird. If you see a handsome lark in a tree, you had better know that he is waiting for a very very pretty little girl who will never come back to him."

The boys cheered and applauded the pretty little girl's cleverness.

"Is your story true?" they cried in unison.

"As true as this old woman's hair is blue," answered my grandmother.

They pleaded for another story, but she told them to go home before the werewolf on the sugar cane cart came out, the one who could smell you from miles away and would come and kill you, unless you ran in a rage through the fields and hollered a list of all his crimes.

Tante Atie's feet pounded the porch a few minutes later.

"Would you read me something?" asked my grandmother.

"I am empty, old woman," she said. "As empty as a dry calabash."

Chapter 19

∧∧∧∧∧∧∧∧∧∧

Tante Atie was very cheerful as she stood in my doorway the next morning.

"Did you sleep all right?" she asked.

She was wearing her I LOVE NEW YORK T-shirt, this time with a long white skirt. Her hair was brushed back and tied in a tiny bun, resting like a porcupine on the back of her neck.

"Are you going somewhere?" I asked.

"Atie speaks to city folks today," she said. "Louise asked me to go with her to have her name put on the archives as having lived in this valley."

My grandmother crept up behind her, gently brushing a broom across the cement.

"What's the use her getting registered?" asked my grandmother. "She is leaving soon, *non*?"

"Her name can be on some piece of paper for future

generations," said Tante Atie. "If people come and they want to know, they will know she lived here."

"People don't need their names on a piece of paper for that," said my grandmother.

"I will list my name too," Tante Atie said.

"If a woman is worth remembering," said my grandmother, "there is no need to have her name carved in letters."

Louise hollered Tante Atie's name from the road.

"That child has lungs like mountain echoes," said my grandmother.

"You have lungs like mountains echoes," she shouted from the house.

Tante Atie rushed out to the porch. My grandmother followed closely behind her. I watched through the window, while Brigitte moved her head in all directions, trying to figure out what all the commotion was about.

Louise was standing in the middle of the road, waiting for Tante Atie. She had on a crisp lavender dress with a butterfly collar. "Atie, you come now," she shouted, ignoring stares from the men on their way to the fields.

"Atie, can't the girl walk up to the house?" asked my grandmother. "We're not a spectacle. You tell her to come to the house. She's frightening the leaves off the trees."

Tante Atie motioned for Louise to come. Louise dashed across the road and entered the yard.

I walked out on the porch with Brigitte. Louise ran up to play with her.

"I remember you," Louise said, grimacing. Brigitte pursed her lips, trying to copy Louise's facial expressions.

The broom fibers whistled as my grandmother furiously raked them in the dust.

"If a person is worth remembering," mumbled my grandmother, "people will remember. It need not be cast in stone."

"We should go," Atie said, taking Louise's arm.

My grandmother went on with her sweeping as Tante Atie and Louise rushed down the road.

My grandmother walked around the yard, collecting sticks and dry leaves. I let her hold Brigitte while I walked across the road to throw some of Brigitte's used diapers over the cliff.

Later, I took my camera out of my suitcase and took a few pictures of my grandmother holding Brigitte.

"They do scare me, those things," she said. "The light in and out. The whole thing is suspect. Seems you can trap somebody's soul in there."

I took a few more shots.

"Now how many is that?" she asked. "Are you afraid that your grandmother will blend into thin air?"

"I want Brigitte to know you when she gets older," I said. "I want her to know how much of each of us is in her."

"Do you suppose she will have any recollection of today?" asked my grandmother.

"You can ask her yourself in a few years."

"If I live so long," she said. "Now go on and put your daughter down. Let her rest a bit."

I took Brigitte inside and laid her down for a nap. While she slept, I looked through my wallet for some pictures that I had brought with me. There was one of Brigitte, all shriveled up, a few hours after she was born. I almost refused to let Joseph take pictures of me with her. I was too ashamed of the stitches on my stomach and the flabs of fat all over my body.

I looked at a small picture of Joseph's and my "wedding."

The two of us were standing before a justice of the peace, a month after we had eloped. I had spent two days in the hospital in Providence and four weeks with stitches between my legs. Joseph could never understand why I had done something so horrible to myself. I could not explain to him that it was like breaking manacles, an act of freedom.

Even though it occurred weeks later, our wedding night was painful. It was like the tearing all over again; the ache and soreness had still not disappeared.

Joseph asked me several times if I really wanted to go through with it. He probably would have understood if I had said no. However, I felt it was my duty as a wife. Something I owed to him, now that he was the only person in the world watching over me. That first very painful time gave us the child.

When Brigitte and I woke up, I took her to the old rocker on the porch. Eliab was flying a kite in the yard. There were a few other colorful kites in the sky, but his was the closest to the ground. He shuffled around a lot, trying to maintain his balance and keep the kite in the air. He slowly released the thread, allowing his kite to venture closer to the clouds.

Another kite swooped down like a vulture. There were pieces of glass and broken razors on the other kite's tail. One of the razors slashed his thread and sent Eliab's kite drifting aimlessly into the breeze. The kite drifted further and further out of sight. Finally it dived down and disappeared, crashing like a lost parachute at an unknown distance.

Eliab reined in his thread. He pulled it with all his might, tying it around the stick as it came to him. The thread suddenly seemed endless. He got tired of coiling, dropped the stick, broke down and cried.

Chapter 20

L ouise came home for supper that night. She brought with her a furless grey pig that looked like a wild rat. My grandmother was cooking in the yard, her fried dumplings sizzling as she turned them over in the pan.

"I brought you one of my pigs," Louise said, holding the animal towards me. "This is one of my smaller ones, a recent born."

"Mèsi mil fwa. How very nice." I said.

"It's a gift, not for money," she said.

Brigitte reached up to grab the pig's brown eyes. Louise quickly pulled the pig away from my daughter's wandering fingers.

"Mèsi," I said. "Thank you very much. Are you listed in the town record book now?"

"Listed for certain," she said. "Atie listed herself and your grandmother too."

Louise gently stroke the pig's back, letting his tail dart across her chin.

"They had this for us at the Poste and Télégramme bureau." Tante Atie pulled an International Express letter out of her satchel.

The letter bore my mother's Nostrand Avenue address.

"Old woman, where's the cassette machine?" shouted Tante Atie.

My grandmother pointed to her room. Tante Atie rushed inside and came back with their cassette player. She laid it on the steps and ripped open the envelope.

My grandmother walked over and sat on the bottom step. She kept her eyes on the clouding sky as my mother's voice came through the small speakers.

"*Allo, Manman*, Atie. Good morning or good night, if it's morning or night. I hope your health is good. Me, you know how it goes. I am swimming with the current. At least I'm not in a mental hospital. I hope you got the money I sent last month, *Manman*. No, I haven't forgotten that little extra you asked me to send, so you can plan your funeral. In any case, there is no hurry. *Manman*, you are still a young woman.

"Speaking of young people, I don't want to trouble your spirits, but I received a telephone call from Sophie's husband not too long ago, telling me that he was on some sort of musical tour. He left Sophie at home with their child and it happens he keeps calling Sophie at their house and she is not there. He is very uneasy."

I wanted to stop the tape, but my grandmother was listening closely, her wrinkled forehead drawn into a knot.

The pig squealed loudly, momentarily drowning out my

mother's voice. My grandmother reached over and yanked the pig's tail. Louise pulled the pig away and buried its face in her chest. The pig whimpered and oinked even louder. Louise placed her hands over its snout and tried to drown out its bawl.

"The husband thought she might have come to spend the time with me. I am already having panic attacks about this. Could be she came to her senses, but not to return to me. I have already lit some candles for her. Green for life, like you've always said."

I tapped the stop button with my toes. The pig began to wail more loudly as though it suddenly felt it could. My grandmother got up and went back to her cooking.

"Isn't it time you reconciled?" Tante Atie said.

Chapter 21

∧∧∧∧∧∧∧∧∧

Louise tied the pig to a pole in the yard. My grandmother fed it a pile of old avocado peels before we ate.

"How much money do you still need to pay for the trip?" I asked Louise.

"I made only ten *gourdes* since the last time you saw me," she said.

Brigitte stretched out her hand to grab the fireflies buzzing around us.

After the meal, we sat on the back porch and listened as Atie read from her notebook.

> She speaks in silent voices, my love.
> Like the cardinal bird, kissing its own image.
> Li *palé vwa mwin,*
> Flapping wings, fallen change
> Broken bottles, whistling snakes

And boom bang drums.
She speaks in silent voices, my love.
I drink her blood with milk
And when the pleasure peaks, my love leaves.

Louise had helped her paraphrase the poem from a book of French poetry that Louise had read when she was still in school.

"You're a poet too," I said to Tante Atie.

She pressed her notebook against her chest.

After her reading, she and Louise strolled into the night, like silhouettes on a picture postcard.

My grandmother took the cassette player to her room to listen to the rest of my mother's message.

I heard my mother's voice coming through the thin walls.

"I am not having the short breath anymore, but every so often, I do find myself dreaming the bad dreams. I thought it would end, but lately it seems to be beginning all over again."

Brigitte was still awake, even after my grandmother fell asleep. I wrapped her in a thick blanket, took her outside to show her the sky. Tante Atie was sitting on the steps feeding the pig.

"Is it male or female?" I asked.

"What difference does it make to the pig?" she asked.

"I want to give it a name."

"Call it Paul or Paulette, Jean or Jeanne. The pig will not

protest. You do not have to name something to make it any more yours."

"Are you in a sour mood?"

"My life, it is nothing," she said.

"What is the matter? Do you miss Croix-des-Rosets?"

"Croix-des-Rosets was painful. Here, though, there is nothing. Nothing at all. The sky seems empty even when I am looking at the moon and stars."

There were drums throbbing in the distance. Some staccato conch shells answered the call.

"I wish I had never left you," I said.

"You did not leave me. You were summoned away. We must graze where we are tied."

"I wish I had stayed with you."

"You must not go back and rearrange your life. It is no use for what has already happened. Sometimes, there is nothing we can do."

"Do you want to go back to Croix-des-Rosets?" I asked.

"I know old people, they have great knowledge. I have been taught never to contradict our elders. I am the oldest child. My place is here. I am supposed to march at the head of the old woman's coffin. I am supposed to lead her funeral procession. But even if lightning should strike me now, I will say this: I am tired. I woke up one morning and I was old myself."

She threw a small green mango at the pig.

"They train you to find a husband," she said. "They poke at your panties in the middle of the night, to see if you are still whole. They listen when you pee, to find out if you're peeing too loud. If you pee loud, it means you've got big spaces between your legs. They make you burn your fingers learning to cook. Then still you have nothing."

The pig jumped up in the air to catch an avocado peel. The jump tightened the cord around its neck, nearly causing it to choke. Tante Atie rushed over and loosened the rope.

"Take your baby inside," she said. "I know you have heard them, the frightening stories of the night."

The pig oinked all night. Tante Atie woke up several times to check on it. My grandmother got up to see what all the commotion was about.

"That Louise causes trouble." My grandmother turned her wrath to Tante Atie. "Everything from her shadow to that pig is trouble."

"Don't trouble me tonight, old woman." Tante Atie strained to control her voice.

The pig started a slow nasal whine.

"I will kill it," said my grandmother. "I will kill it."

My daughter woke up with a sharp cry.

I fed her and rocked her back to sleep. The pig, it was still crying, but there was nothing I could do.

Louise was out of breath when she ran up to the house the next morning. Her face was reddened with tears and her blouse soaked with sweat.

My grandmother motioned for me to take the baby inside the house. I backed myself into the doorway while clinging tightly to my daughter.

I watched from the threshold as Tante Atie gave Louise a cup of cold water from the jug beneath the porch.

"Li allé. It's over," Louise said, panting as though she had both asthma and the hiccups at the same time. "They killed Dessalines."

"Who killed Dessalines?" asked my grandmother.

"The *Macoutes* killed Dessalines."

Louise buried her head in Tante Atie's shoulder. Their faces were so close that their lips could meet if they both turned at the same time.

"Calm now," said Tante Atie, as she massaged Louise's scalp.

"That's why I need to go," sobbed Louise. "I need to leave."

"A poor man is dead and all you can think about is your journey," snapped my grandmother.

"Next might be me or you with the *Macoutes*," said Louise.

"We already had our turn," said my grandmother. "Sophie, you keep the child behind the threshold. You are not to bring her out until that restless spirit is in the ground."

In the fairy tales, the *Tonton Macoute* was a bogeyman, a scarecrow with human flesh. He wore denim overalls and carried a cutlass and a knapsack made of straw. In his knapsack, he always had scraps of naughty children, whom he dismembered to eat as snacks. *If you don't respect your elders, then the Tonton Macoute will take you away.*

Outside the fairy tales, they roamed the streets in broad daylight, parading their Uzi machine guns.

Who invented the Macoutes? The devil didn't do it and God didn't do it.

Ordinary criminals walked naked in the night. They

slicked their bodies with oil so they could slip through most fingers. But the *Macoutes*, they did not hide. When they entered a house, they asked to be fed, demanded the woman of the house, and forced her into her own bedroom. Then all you heard was screams until it was her daughter's turn. If a mother refused, they would make her sleep with her son and brother or even her own father.

My father might have been a *Macoute*. He was a stranger who, when my mother was sixteen years old, grabbed her on her way back from school. He dragged her into the cane fields, and pinned her down on the ground. He had a black bandanna over his face so she never saw anything but his hair, which was the color of eggplants. He kept pounding her until she was too stunned to make a sound. When he was done, he made her keep her face in the dirt, threatening to shoot her if she looked up.

For months she was afraid that he would creep out of the night and kill her in her sleep. She was terrified that he would come and tear out the child growing inside her. At night, she tore her sheets and bit off pieces of her own flesh when she had nightmares.

My grandmother sent her to a rich mulatto family in Croix-des-Rosets to do any work she could for free room and board, as a rèstavèk. Even though my mother was pregnant and half insane, the family took her in anyway because my grandmother had cooked and cleaned in their house for years, before she married my grandfather.

My mother came back to Dame Marie after I was born. She tried to kill herself several times when I was a baby. The nightmares were just too real. Tante Atie took care of me.

The rich mulatto family helped my mother apply for

papers to get out of Haiti. It took four years before she got her visa, but by the time she began to recover her sanity, she left.

Tante Atie took me to Croix-des-Rosets, so I could go to school. And when I left, she moved back here, to Dame Marie, to take care of my grandmother.

Somehow Dessalines's death brought to mind all those frightening memories. My grandmother would not let me take Brigitte outside until Dessalines was laid to rest in the ground. That night, I opened the window to listen to the night breeze rustling through the dry *tcha tcha* bean pods in the distance.

Tante Atie was talking to Louise. Her voice was muffled, her breathing quickened, as she sobbed loudly.

"It is the calm and silent waters that drown you. I never thought it would make me so sad to look in Sophie's face."

The pig gave a sudden cry as Louise rushed away. Tante Atie slipped inside the house through a side door.

"Nothing should have taken you out into that black night." My grandmother was waiting inside. "Did a bird nest in your hair? You seem to have lost your mind."

"Maybe a good death would save me from all this," Tante Atie said.

I heard a thump, like a slap across the face.

Tante Atie stormed out of the house and marched out to the porch.

When I came out, Tante Atie was sitting with a lamp and her notebook on her lap. I folded the flaps of Joseph's shirt between my legs and sat on the top step next to her.

"Do you ever visit Mr. Augustin?" I asked.

"No," she said. "Sometimes people just disappear from our lives and it is not a bad thing."

We sat silently and looked at the stars for a while.

"I am going to excuse myself and go back inside," I said. "I do not want to leave the baby alone for long."

"The old woman, she is going to send word to your mother that you are here," she said.

"My mother does not concern herself with where I am."

"You are judging her much too harshly."

"When Joseph and I first married, I used to write her every month. I have sent her pictures of Brigitte. She keeps the letters, but makes no reply."

"She will come," said Tante Atie.

"Come where?"

"She will come here. She has promised for a long time to come and arrange the old woman's funeral and the old woman will place on the cassette words begging her to come, so you can settle this quarrel."

Brigitte got up early the next morning, ready to bounce and play. I lay her on the bed and tried to make her do some baby exercises.

In the next room, my grandmother was recording her reply cassette to my mother.

"Martine, *ki jan ou yé?*" How are you? "We are doing fine here, following in the shadow of Father Time. I am well, except for the old bones that ache sometime. Dessalines has died. *Macoutes* kill him. Do you remember him? He was the coal man.

"I don't even need to talk about Atie. She is carrying on like she has got a pound of rocks on her chest. Sadness is now her way of life. You needn't worry about Sophie. Could be she is on a little holiday. The bird, it always returns to the nest."

My grandmother stopped to clear her throat. Brigitte grabbed my fingers and held them tightly as she rolled on her side.

"Is Atie in her room?" yelled my grandmother.

"She is out!" I shouted back.

Brigitte shrieked, trying to scream along.

"Is there something you want to say to your mother?"

"No!"

The recorder clicked to a stop.

"Any more you want to say?" asked my grandmother.

"I think we've already said enough."

In the distance, the bells tolled, announcing Dessalines's funeral. Tante Atie stumbled into her room, her body rocking from side to side. She lowered herself to the ground, her large feet barely sidestepping my outstretched leg and Brigitte's toes. Tante Atie's eyes were red; she blinked quickly trying to keep them open. She snapped her fingers and made faces at Brigitte, to get her attention.

"Are you all right?" I asked her.

"Fine, good."

Her breath smelled like rum. She stretched her body out on the floor and within a few seconds, fell asleep.

She woke up at noon with a panic-stricken look in her eyes.

"My notebook?" she asked. "You seen it?"

I shook my head no. Brigitte was asleep on the bed. I was

afraid that Tante Atie's sudden movements would wake her up.

"Maybe the book's in my room," she mumbled, heading for the door.

"Were you drinking?" I asked.

"I drink a little to forget my troubles," she said. "It's no more a vice than the old woman and her tobacco."

She walked out to the yard, splashed some water over her face, then started towards the road.

She came back in the very early morning hours. The voices in the yard kept me awake.

"You can go now," said Tante Atie.

"Let me see you enter," insisted Louise. "That calf of yours, go and rest that calf of yours."

"People do not die from aching calves," said Tante Atie. "You think I am an old lady. I do not need a walking cane."

"Be pleasant, Atie. Go inside."

I heard Tante Atie walk inside.

The bed squealed under her body as she crashed on it. Louise walked home alone in the fading dusk.

Chapter 22

∧∧∧∧∧∧∧∧∧

The next morning, a pack of rainbow butterflies hovered around the porch. I was sitting on the steps, watching the sun rise behind the shack spotted hills.

My grandmother's face was powdered with ashes as she left the house. Walking past me, she tapped my knee with the tip of her cane. She lowered a black veil over her face as she twirled a rosary between her fingers.

The baby let out a sudden cry from Tante Atie's room. I rushed back in. Tante Atie was pacing as she carried her around the room. Brigitte stretched out her hands when she saw me. She pressed her face down on my neck when I held her against my body.

"Did the old woman leave for the cemetery?" Tante Atie asked.

"Is that where she's going?"

"She is going to pay her last respects to Dessalines."

Brigitte clawed my neck with her fingernails.

"You and Louise, you are very close, aren't you?" I asked Tante Atie.

"When you have a good friend," she said, "you must hold her with both hands."

"It will be hard for you when she leaves, won't it?"

"I will miss her like my own skin."

My grandmother had her veil on her arm as she walked back towards the house. Eliab ran to her and took a heavy bundle from her hand. He pulled out its contents, sniffing the coconuts before setting them down.

"Did you have a nice visit to the cemetery?" I asked.

"There are two ways to go to the cemetery. One is on your two feet, the other is in a box. Each way, it is a large travail. Where is your Tante Atie?"

"She is visiting with Louise."

"Why do I even ask?"

She picked up a machete from under the porch and chopped a green coconut in half. Eliab pushed an open gourd beneath the coconut and caught the cloudy liquid flowing out of it. My grandmother carved out the flesh with a spoon and stuffed it in her mouth.

She chopped another coconut and brought it over to me. The coconut milk spilled all over my chest as I raised the shell to my lips.

My daughter reached up to grab the coconut. My grandmother and Eliab sat on an old tree stump, sharing the soft mush inside the coconut. My grandmother threw some at the pig, which it leaped up to swallow.

Tante Atie did not come home for supper. My grandmother and I ate in the yard, while Brigitte slept in a blanket in my arms. My grandmother was watching a light move between two distant points on the hill.

"Do you see that light moving yonder?" she asked, pointing to the traveling lantern. "Do you know why it goes to and fro like that?"

She was concentrating on the shift, her pupils traveling with each movement.

"It is a baby," she said, "a baby is being born. The midwife is taking trips from the shack to the yard where the pot is boiling. Soon we will know whether it is a boy or a girl."

"How will we know that?"

"If it is a boy, the lantern will be put outside the shack. If there is a man, he will stay awake all night with the new child."

"What if it is a girl?"

"If it is a girl, the midwife will cut the child's cord and go home. Only the mother will be left in the darkness to hold her child. There will be no lamps, no candles, no more light."

We waited. The light went out in the house about an hour later. By that time, my grandmother had dozed off. Another little girl had come into the world.

Chapter 23

∧·∨·∨·∧·∨·∧·∨·∧

A rooster crowed at the next morning's dawn. I peeked into Tante Atie's room. Her bed was still made, without a wrinkle on it. She had not come home at all the night before. My grandmother made herself some bitter black coffee with a lump of salt to prepare her body for the shock of bad news.

I sat out on the porch with Brigitte waiting for the food vendors to come by. They trickled by slowly, each chanting the names and praises of their merchandise.

My grandmother bought some bananas, boiled eggs, and hard biscuits.

Louise and Tante Atie came up the road. Tante Atie was ahead. Louise marched a few feet behind her.

My grandmother looked up without acknowledging their presence. Louise walked into the yard, charged towards the tree, untied her pig, picked it up, and walked away.

"Why? What are you doing?" I called after her.

She did not turn back.

"What is the matter with her?" I asked Tante Atie.

"*Manman* told her to come get the pig or she would kill it," Tante Atie said.

Tante Atie was carrying a small jar of water with three leeches inside.

"Is it true Grandmè Ifé? Did you say that?" I asked.

"We need a pig, we buy a pig," said my grandmother.

"I will buy it," I said.

"*Non non*," Tante Atie jumped quickly. "The money, it will surely go for her boat trip to Miami."

"You think you can keep money out of her hands?" asked my grandmother.

"I do not want to push her into the ocean," Tante Atie said.

She raised the leech jar towards the sun. The animals squirmed away from the light, their black slippery bodies coiling into small balls. She raised her skirt and stretched out her calf. Opening the jar, she tipped it over so that the water was soaking her skin. The leeches slowly crawled out of the jar and climbed on a lump on her calf.

She ground her teeth when one of the larger leeches bit into her skin. She leaned back against the porch railing, pulled her notebook from her sack, and began writing her name. She wrote it over and over, following a pattern at the top of the page.

The leeches sucked the blood out of her lump, until they were plump and full. She pulled them away one by one, slid her fingers down their backs, and pumped the blood into an empty jar. I felt my head spinning, my stomach about to turn inside out. Tante Atie noticed the pained expression on my face.

"It's no loss, angel," she said. "It's only blood, bad blood at that."

I asked my grandmother if I could cook supper for us that night.

Tante Atie offered to take me to a private vendor where food was cheaper than the *maché*. She put the leeches in some clean water and we started down the road.

"What are you making for us?" she asked.

"Rice, black beans, and herring sauce," I said.

"Your mother's favorite meal."

"That's what we cooked most often."

We followed a footpath off the road, down to a shallow stream. An old mule was yanking water vines from the edge of the stream while baby crabs freely dashed around its nostrils.

A woman filled a calabash a few feet from where my sandals muddied the water. Tante Atie chatted with the women as she went by. Some young girls were sitting barechested in the water, the sun casting darker shadows into their faces. Their hands squirted blackened suds as they pounded their clothes with water rocks.

A dusty footpath led us to a tree-lined cemetery at the top of the hill. Tante Atie walked between the wooden crosses, collecting the bamboo skeletons of fallen kites. She stepped around the plots where empty jars, conch shells, and marbles served as grave markers.

"Walk straight," said Tante Atie, "you are in the presence of family."

She walked around to each plot, and called out the names of all those who had been buried there. There was my great-grandmother, Beloved Martinelle Brigitte. Her sister, My First Joy Sophilus Gentille. My grandfather's sister, My Hope Atinia Ifé, and finally my grandfather, Charlemagne Le Grand Caco.

Tante Atie named them all on sight.

"Our family name, Caco, it is the name of a scarlet bird. A bird so crimson, it makes the reddest hibiscus or the brightest flame trees seem white. The Caco bird, when it dies, there is always a rush of blood that rises to its neck and the wings, they look so bright, you would think them on fire."

From the cemetery, we took a narrow footpath to the vendor's hut. On either side of us were wild grasses that hissed as though they were full of snakes.

We walked to a whitewashed shack where a young woman sold rice and black beans from the same sisal mat where she slept with her husband.

In the yard, the husband sat under the shade of a straw parasol with a pipe in his mouth and a demijohn at his feet. He was pounding small nails into leather straps and thin layers of polished wood to make sandals.

The hammering echoed in my head until I reached the cane fields. The men were singing about a woman who flew without her skin at night, and when she came back home, she found her skin peppered and could not put it back on. Her husband had done it to teach her a lesson. He ended up killing her.

. . .

I was surprised how fast it came back. The memory of how everything came together to make a great meal. The fragrance of the spices guided my fingers the way no instructions or measurements could.

Haitian men, they insist that their women are virgins and have their ten fingers.

According to Tante Atie, each finger had a purpose. It was the way she had been taught to prepare herself to become a woman. Mothering. Boiling. Loving. Baking. Nursing. Frying. Healing. Washing. Ironing. Scrubbing. It wasn't her fault, she said. Her ten fingers had been named for her even before she was born. Sometimes, she even wished she had six fingers on each hand so she could have two left for herself.

I rushed back and forth between the iron pots in the yard. The air smelled like spices that I had not cooked with since I'd left my mother's home two years before.

I usually ate random concoctions: frozen dinners, samples from global cookbooks, food that was easy to put together and brought me no pain. No memories of a past that at times was cherished and at others despised.

By the time we ate, the air was pregnant with rain. Thunder groaned in the starless sky while the lanterns flickered in the hills.

"Well done," Tante Atie said after her fourth serving of my rice and beans.

My grandmother chewed slowly as she gave my daughter her bottle.

"If the wood is well carved," said my grandmother, "it teaches us about the carpenter. Atie, you taught Sophie well."

Tante Atie was taken off guard by my grandmother's compliment. She kissed me on the forehead before taking the dishes to the yard to wash. Then, she went into the house, took her notebook, and left for her lesson with Louise.

My grandmother groaned her disapproval. She pulled out a small pouch and packed pinches of tobacco powder into her nose. She inhaled deeply, stuffing more and more into her nostrils.

She had a look of deep concern on her face, as her eyes surveyed the evening clouds.

"*Tandé*. Do you hear anything?" she asked.

There was nothing but the usual night sounds: birds finding their ways in the dark, as they shuffled through the leaves.

Often at night, there were women who travelled long distances, on foot or on mare, to save the car fare to Port-au-Prince.

I strained my eyes to see beyond the tree shadows on the road.

"There is a girl going home," my grandmother said. "You cannot see her. She is far away. Quite far. It is not the distance that is important. If I hear a girl from far away, there is an emotion, something that calls to my soul. If your soul is linked with someone, somehow you can always feel when something is happening to them."

"Is it Tante Atie, the girl on the road?"

"*Non*. It is really a girl. A younger woman."

"Is the girl in danger?"

"That's why you listen. You should hear young feet crushing wet leaves. Her feet make a *swish-swash* when they

152

hit the ground and when she hurries, it sounds like a whip chasing a mule."

I listened closely, but heard no whip.

"When it is dark, all men are black," she said. "There is no way to know anything unless you apply your ears. When you listen, it's kòm si you had deafness before and you can hear now. Sometimes you can't fall asleep because the sound of someone crying keeps you awake. A whisper sounds like a roar to your ears. Your ears are witness to matters that do not concern you. And what is worse, you cannot forget. Now, listen. Her feet make a swish sound and when she hurries it's like a whip in the wind."

I tried, but I heard no whip.

"It's the way old men cry," she said. "Grown brave men have a special way they cry when they are afraid."

She closed her eyes and lowered her head to concentrate.

"It is Ti Alice," she said.

"Who is Ti Alice?"

"The young child in the bushes, it is Ti Alice. Someone is there with her."

"Is she in danger?"

My grandmother tightened her eyelids.

"I know Ti Alice," she said. "I know her mother."

"Why is she in the bushes?"

"She must be fourteen or fifteen years now."

"Why is she out there?"

"She is rushing back to her mother. She was with a friend, a boy."

I thought I heard a few hushed whispers.

"I think I hear a little," I said, rocking my daughter with excitement.

"Ti Alice and the boy, they are bidding one another good-bye, for the night."

My grandmother wrapped her arms around her body, rocking and cradling herself.

"What is happening now?" I asked.

"Her mother is waiting for her at the door of their hut. She is pulling her inside to test her."

The word sent a chill through my body.

"She is going to test to see if young Alice is still a virgin," my grandmother said. "The mother, she will drag her inside the hut, take her last small finger and put it inside her to see if it goes in. You said the other night that your mother tested you. That is what is now happening to Ti Alice."

I have heard it compared to a virginity cult, our mothers' obsession with keeping us pure and chaste. My mother always listened to the echo of my urine in the toilet, for if it was too loud it meant that I had been deflowered. I learned very early in life that virgins always took small steps when they walked. They never did acrobatic splits, never rode horses or bicycles. They always covered themselves well and, even if their lives depended on it, never parted with their panties.

The story goes that there was once an extremely rich man who married a poor black girl. He had chosen her out of hundreds of prettier girls because she was untouched. For the wedding night, he bought her the whitest sheets and nightgowns he could possibly find. For himself, he bought a can of thick goat milk in which he planned to sprinkle a drop of her hymen blood to drink.

Then came their wedding night. The girl did not bleed. The man had his honor and reputation to defend. He could not face the town if he did not have a blood-spotted sheet to hang in his courtyard the next morning. He did the best he could to make her bleed, but no matter how hard he tried, the girl did not bleed. So he took a knife and cut her between her legs to get some blood to show. He got enough blood for her wedding gown and sheets, an unusual amount to impress the neighbors. The blood kept flowing like water out of the girl. It flowed so much it wouldn't stop. Finally, drained of all her blood, the girl died.

Later, during her funeral procession, her blood-soaked sheets were paraded by her husband to show that she had been a virgin on her wedding night. At the grave site, her husband drank his blood-spotted goat milk and cried like a child.

I closed my eyes upon the images of my mother slipping her hand under the sheets and poking her pinky at a void, hoping that it would go no further than the length of her fingernail.

Like Tante Atie, she had told me stories while she was doing it, weaving elaborate tales to keep my mind off the finger, which I knew one day would slip into me and condemn me. I had learned to *double* while being *tested*. I would close my eyes and imagine all the pleasant things that I had known. The lukewarm noon breeze through our bougainvillea. Tante Atie's gentle voice blowing over a field of daffodils.

There were many cases in our history where our ancestors had *doubled*. Following in the *vaudou* tradition, most of our presidents were actually one body split in two: part flesh and part shadow. That was the only way they could murder and rape so many people and still go home to play with their children and make love to their wives.

After my marriage, whenever Joseph and I were together, I *doubled*.

"The testing? Why do the mothers do that?" I asked my grandmother.

"If a child dies, you do not die. But if your child is disgraced, you are disgraced. And people, they think daughters will be raised trash with no man in the house."

"Did your mother do this to you?"

"From the time a girl begins to menstruate to the time you turn her over to her husband, the mother is responsible for her purity. If I give a soiled daughter to her husband, he can shame my family, speak evil of me, even bring her back to me."

"When you tested my mother and Tante Atie, couldn't you tell that they hated it?"

"I had to keep them clean until they had husbands."

"But they don't have husbands."

"The burden was not mine alone."

"I hated the tests," I said. "It is the most horrible thing that ever happened to me. When my husband is with me now, it gives me such nightmares that I have to bite my tongue to do it again."

"With patience, it goes away."

"No Grandmè Ifé, it does not."

"Ti Alice, she has passed her examination."

The sky reddened with a sudden flash of lightning. "Now

you have a child of your own. You must know that everything a mother does, she does for her child's own good. You cannot always carry the pain. You must liberate yourself."

We walked to my room and put my daughter down to sleep.

"I will go soon," I told my grandmother, "back to my husband."

"It is better," she said. "It is hard for a woman to raise girls alone."

She walked into her room, took her statue of Erzulie, and pressed it into my hand.

"My heart, it weeps like a river," she said, "for the pain we have caused you."

I held the statue against my chest as I cried in the night. I thought I heard my grandmother crying too, but it was the rain slowing down to a mere drizzle, tapping on the roof.

The next morning, I went jogging, along the road, through the cemetery plot, and into the hills. The sun had already dried some of the puddles from the drizzle the night before.

Along the way, people stared at me with puzzled expressions on their faces. *Is this what happens to our girls when they leave this place?* They become such frightened creatures that they run like the wind, from nothing at all.

157

Chapter 24

∧∧∧∧∧∧∧∧∧

Three days later, my mother came. When I first caught a glimpse of her, she was sitting on the back of a cart being pulled by two teenage boys.

Eliab raced to the yard, grabbed my grandmother's hand, and yanked her towards the road.

My mother was shielding her face from us, hiding behind a red umbrella.

My grandmother followed Eliab to the edge of the road.

"That lady," Eliab said, pointing at the umbrella guarding my mother's face. "That lady, she says she belongs to you."

Tante Atie was in the yard boiling some water for our morning coffee. She got up quickly when my grandmother started screaming my mother's name.

"Min Martine!"

"Tololo. Tololo," Eliab chimed in as though it was his long-lost mother who had come back.

My grandmother grabbed her broom and speared it in the ground to anchor herself.

My mother folded the red umbrella and laid it on top of a large suitcase on the cart next to her.

Some of the road vendors gathered around her to say hello.

My mother kissed them on the cheek and stroked their children's heads. They looked curiously at her cerise jumper, ballooned around her small frame.

My grandmother was trembling on the spot where she was standing. Tante Atie put her hands on her hips and stared ahead. She did not look the least bit surprised.

A plantain green scarf floated in the breeze behind my mother. She skipped through the dust and rushed across the yard. Eliab circled around her like a wingless butterfly.

My mother walked over and kissed my grandmother. Tante Atie moved slowly towards her, not particularly excited. My mother was glowing.

Tante Atie tapped her lips against my mother's cheeks, then went back to fanning the cooking sticks with my grandmother's hat.

"*Sak pasé*, Atie?" asked my mother.

"You," answered Tante Atie fanning the flames. "You're what's new."

I clung to the porch railing as my anchor. It had been almost two years since the last time we saw each other. My mother's skin was unusually light, a pale mocha, three or four shades lighter than any of ours.

Brigitte's body tightened, as though she could sense the tension in mine.

"I see you still wear the *deuil*," my mother said to my grandmother.

"It is all the same," answered my grandmother. "The black is easier; it does not get dirty."

"*Mon Dieu*, you do not look bad for an old lady," said my mother. "And you have been talking about arranging your funeral like it was tomorrow."

"Your skin looks lighter," said my grandmother. "Is it *prodwi*? You use something?"

My mother looked embarrassed.

"It is very cold in America," my mother said. "The cold turns us into ghosts."

"Papa Shango, the sun here, will change that," my grandmother said.

"I am not staying long enough for that," my mother said. "When I got your telegram, I decided to come and see Sophie and take care of your affairs at the same time. I plan to stay for only three days. This is not the visit I owe you. This is just circumstance. When I come again, I will stay with you for a very long time."

I watched her from the railing, waiting for her to look over and address me personally.

She looked very young and thin, but for the most part healthy. Because of the roomy size of her jumper, I couldn't tell whether or not she was wearing her prosthetic bra.

"Sophie, walk to your mother," said my grandmother.

They were all staring at me, even Eliab. My mother put her hands in her pockets. She narrowed her eyes as she tried to see my face through the sun's glare.

Brigitte began to twist in my arms. She sensed something.

"Sophie, walk to your mother." My grandmother's voice grew more forceful.

My mother looked uncomfortable, almost scared.

I did not move. We stared at each other across the yard, each waiting for the other to yield. As her daughter, I was expected to walk over and greet her first. However, I did not trust my legs. I wasn't sure I could make it down the steps without slipping and hurting both myself and Brigitte.

"Walk to your mother." My grandmother was becoming angry.

"It is okay," my mother said, coming towards me. "I will walk to her."

She climbed onto the porch and kissed me on the cheek.

Brigitte reached up to grab a large loop earring on my mother's right lobe.

"You didn't send word you were coming," I said.

"Let me see her," she said, extending her hands for Brigitte. Brigitte leaned forward. I let her slip into my mother's grasp.

"How old is she now?" she asked.

"Almost six months."

She made funny faces at Brigitte.

"I got all the pictures you sent me," she said.

"Why didn't you answer?"

"I couldn't find the words," she said. "How are you?"

"I've been better."

She went back to the yard to pay the cart boys and took Brigitte with her.

"You're not staying here, are you?" she asked when she came back to the porch.

She tickled Brigitte's armpits as she spoke, giggling along with her.

I reached for my daughter. She pressed Brigitte's body against her chest and would not give her back.

"*Manman* asked me to come here and make things better between us. It's not right for a mother and daughter to be enemies. *Manman* thinks it puts a curse on the family. Besides, your husband came to me and I could not refuse him."

"You've seen him?"

"Oh, the flames in your eyes."

"How is he?"

"Worried. I told him we would be back in three days."

"You can't make plans for me."

"I did."

We were speaking to one another in English without realizing it.

"Oh that *cling-clang* talk," interrupted my grandmother. "It sounds like glass breaking."

Brigitte was pulling at my mother's earrings. My mother took them off and handed them to me.

"You and I, we started wrong," my mother said. "You are now a woman, with your own house. We are allowed to start again."

The mid-morning sky looked like an old quilt, with long bands of red and indigo stretching their way past drifting clouds. Like everything else, eventually even the rainbows disappeared.

Chapter 25

/\/\/\/\/\/\/\/\

M y mother changed into a sun dress to parcel out what she had brought. Under the spaghetti straps, I could see the true unbleached ebony shade of her skin. In contrast, her face looked like the palm of a hand.

My grandmother reached over and cupped her hands over my mother's prosthetic bra.

"Do they hurt?" asked my grandmother.

"No," my mother answered, "because they are not really part of me."

She had brought cloth for my mother and Tante Atie to share. Packaged rice and beans and packaged spices for my grandmother.

I got the diapers and underclothes that Joseph had sent for the baby, along with some T-shirts and shorts for me.

"If you were not such a stubborn old woman," my mother said to my grandmother, "I would move you and

Atie to Croix-des-Rosets or the city. I could buy you a bougainvillea. You would have electricity, and all kinds of modern machines."

"I like myself here," said my grandmother. "I need to see about my papers for this land and I need to have all the things for my passing. With all my children here, this is a good time."

Tante Atie was writing in her notebook. My mother leaned over to look. Tante Atie pulled her notebook away and slammed it shut.

"We will see the notary about the land papers," said my grandmother. "We will do it tomorrow."

"What will you do with the land?" asked Tante Atie.

"I want to make the papers show all the people it belongs to."

Tante Atie did not go to Louise's house, but spent the evening in the yard, staring at the sky.

My mother could not sleep. She went outside and sat with Tante Atie. They looked up for a long time without saying a word.

Finally my mother said, "Do you remember all the unpleasant stories Manman used to tell us about the stars in the sky?"

"My favorite," said Tante Atie, "was the one about the girl who wished she could marry a star and then went up there and, as real as her eyes were black, the man she wished for was a monster."

"Atie, you remember everything."

"I liked what Papa said better. He thought, Papa, that the stars were brave men."

"Maybe he was right," my mother said.

"He said they would come back and fall in love with me. I wouldn't say that was right."

"We used to fight so hard when we saw a star wink. You said it was winking at you. I thought it was winking at me. I think, *Manman*, she told us that unpleasant story about the stars to stop the quarrels."

"Young girls, they should be allowed to keep their pleasant stories," Tante Atie said.

"Why don't you sleep in your bed?" asked my mother.

"Because it is empty in my bed."

"You had *flanneurs*, men who came to ask for your hand."

"Until better women came along."

"How could you not be chosen? You are Atie Caco."

"Atie Caco to you. Special to no one."

"You were so beautiful, Atie, when you were a girl. Papa, he loved you best."

"I have then the curse of a girl whose papa loved her best."

Tante Atie rubbed the scar on the side of her head. They looked up at the sky and pointed to a blinking star.

"You can keep the brightest ones," said Tante Atie. "When you are gone, I will have them all to myself."

"We come from a place," my mother said, "where in one instant, you can lose your father and all your other dreams."

Chapter 26

∧∨∧∨∧∨∧∨∧∨∧

My mother and grandmother left early for the notary's. Tante Atie was not in her room. Eliab was playing with pieces of brown paper, stuffing them with leaves to make cigars.

I called him to buy me some milk from the market.

"The new lady," he said, "does she belong to you?"

"Sometimes I claim her," I said, "sometimes I do not."

I gave him some money to buy me some goat milk from the market. He came back with some milk in a cut-off plastic container and a large mango for himself.

"That young fellow, he wants to marry your daughter," my grandmother said as she and my mother walked into the yard.

Eliab looked embarrassed.

"Does that fellow know?" my mother laughed. "My daughter has a very old husband."

My mother was carrying a few large bundles.

I had never seen my grandmother so happy. My mother was glowing.

"We are now landowners," my mother said. "We all now own part of La Nouvelle Dame Marie."

"Did this land not always belong to you and Tante Atie?" I asked my mother.

"Yes, but now you have a piece of it too."

She flashed the new deed for the house.

"*La terre sera également divisée*," she read the document. "Equally, my dear. The land is equally divided between Atie and me and you and your daughter."

My grandmother pulled out a dressy church hat that she had bought for Tante Atie.

"Sunday we go to the cathedral," said my mother. "We meet *Manman's* priest."

My mother kissed the bottom of Brigitte's feet.

"Where is Atie?" asked my mother. "I got her a hat that will make her look downright chic."

"She went out," I said.

"The gods will punish me for Atie's ways." My grandmother moaned.

Tante Atie kept her eyes on the lantern on the hills as we ate dinner that night. She was squinting as though she wanted to see with her ears, like my grandmother.

"I look forward to the Mass on Sunday," my grandmother said, breaking the silence. "I want that young priest. The one they call Lavalas. I want him to sing the last song at my funeral."

Brigitte shook the new rattle that my mother had brought her.

My grandmother took Brigitte from me and put a few rice grains in her mouth. My daughter opened her mouth wide, trying to engulf the rice.

Tante Atie walked up the steps and went back to her room.

"I don't know," my grandmother said. "Her mood changes more than the colors in the sky. Take her with you when you return to New York."

"I have asked her before," my mother said. "She wants to be with you."

"She feels she must," my grandmother said. "It's not love. It is duty."

Everything was rustling in Tante Atie's room, as though she were packing. She was mumbling to herself so I dared not peek in. In the yard my mother and grandmother were sitting around the table, passing my grandmother's old clay pipe back and forth to each other.

"*Manman*, will you know when your time comes to die?" my mother asked sadly.

"The old bones, they will know."

"I want to be buried here when I die," my mother said.

"You should tell Sophie. She is your daughter. She will respect your wishes."

"I don't want much," my mother said. "I don't want a Mass like you. I want to be buried the day after I die. Just like the old days when we kept our dead home."

"That is reason for you and Sophie to be friends," my

grandmother said. "She can carry out your wishes. I can help, but she is your child."

My mother paced the corridor most of the night. She walked into my room and tiptoed over to my bed. I crossed my legs tightly, already feeling my body shivering.

I shut my eyes tightly and pretended to be asleep.

She walked over to the baby and stood over her for a long time. Tears streamed down her face as she watched us sleep. The tears came harder. She turned and walked out.

My mother walked into the room at dawn while I was changing Brigitte's diapers.

"Are you all right?" I asked.

"Fine," she said.

"Do you still have trouble sleeping?" I tried to be polite.

"It's worse when I am here," she said.

"Are you having nightmares?"

"More than ever," she said.

My old sympathy was coming back. I remembered the nightmares. Sometimes, I even had some myself. I was feeling sorry for her.

"I thought it was my face that brought them on," I said.

"Your face?"

"Because I look like him. My father. A child out of wedlock always looks like its father."

She seemed shocked that I remembered.

"When I first saw you in New York, I must admit, it frightened me the way you looked. But it is not something that I can help. It is not something that you can help. It is just part of our lives.

"As a woman, your face has changed. You are a different person. Besides, I have always had nightmares. Every night of my life. It was just stronger then, because that was the first time I was seeing that face."

"Why did you put me through those tests?" I blurted out.

"If I tell you today, you must never ask me again."

I wanted to reserve my right to ask as many times as I needed to. I was not angry with her anymore. I had a greater need to understand, so that I would never repeat it myself.

"I did it," she said, "because my mother had done it to me. I have no greater excuse. I realize standing here that the two greatest pains of my life are very much related. The one good thing about my being raped was that it made the testing stop. The testing and the rape. I live both every day."

"You're not dressed yet?" My grandmother was standing in the doorway. "I am ready to go."

My mother placed her hand on my grandmother's shoulder and signaled for her to wait. She turned back to me and said in English, "I want to be your friend, your very very good friend, because you saved my life many times when you woke me up from those nightmares."

My mother went to my grandmother's room to dress and soon they left for the road.

They came back a few hours later with a pan full of bloody pig meat.

In our family, we had come to expect that people can disappear into thin air. All traces lost except in the vivid eyes of one's memory. Still, Tante Atie had never thought that Louise would leave her so quickly, without any last words.

That night, Tante Atie had a glazed look on her face as she ate the fried pork.

"Forgive me if I don't go to Mass ever again. I will choke on the Communion if I take it angry."

Louise had sold her pig, taken my grandmother's money, and left the valley, without so much as a good-bye to Tante Atie.

Chapter 27

∧∨∧∨∧∨∧∨∧∨

I asked Tante Atie if Brigitte and I could sleep in her room with her, the night before we were to return to New York. We put down some sheets on the floor and stretched out with the baby between us.

Tante Atie turned her back to the wall as though she did not want me to see her cry. We heard my mother pacing the front room's floor, back and forth waiting for the sun to rise.

"Louise would have found her money, somehow, someway," I told Tante Atie. "She would have done anything to make that trip. Sometimes, when people have something they want to do, you cannot stop them. Even if you want to."

"I was a fool to think she was my friend," Tante Atie said. "Money makes dogs dance."

"At least she taught you how to read your letters."

"Anyone could have taught me that. A lot of good letters will do me now."

"Sometimes I wish I could go back in time with you, to when we were younger."

She closed her eyes, as though to drift off to sleep.

"The past is always the past," she said. "Children are the rewards of life and you were my child."

The next day, Tante Atie led the cart that took my mother's and my bags to the marketplace. The sun was shining in Tante Atie's eyes as she carried my daughter for me. My grandmother and my mother had their arms wrapped around one another's waists, clinging as though they would never see each other again.

When we got to the van that would take us to Port-au-Prince, my grandmother just stepped back and let go. My mother kissed her on both cheeks and then walked over and kissed Tante Atie. Tante Atie tapped my mother's shoulder and whispered for her to be careful.

As Tante Atie handed me my daughter, she said, "Treat your mother well, you don't have her forever."

My grandmother tapped the baby's chin.

"The faces in this child," she said, fighting back her tears.

My mother paid the *tap tap* driver for us to have the van all to ourselves. It was all ours except for the old hunchback, whose charcoal bags had already been loaded on it.

Tante Atie was standing under the red *flamboyant* tree, clinging to a low branch as the van pulled away. Slowly, everything in Dame Marie became a blur. My grandmother and the vendors. Tante Atie at the flaming red tree. The *Macoutes* around Louise's stand. Even the hill in the distance, the place that Tante Atie called Guinea. A place where all the women in my family hoped to eventually meet one another, at the very end of each of our journeys.

Four

⋀⋀⋀⋀⋀⋀⋀

Chapter 28

∧∧∧∧∧∧∧∧∧∧∧∧

I t was a rocky ride to the airport. The old hunchback lowered her body onto a sack of charcoal to sleep, as though it were a feather mattress. My mother kept her eyes on the barren hills speeding outside the window. I wished there were other people with us, chatty *Madan Saras*, vendors, to add some teeth sucking and laughter to our journey.

My mother reached over and grabbed the cloth bells on Brigitte's booties, sadly ignoring the skeletal mares and even bonier women tugging their beasts to open markets along the route.

In the city, we were slowed down by the heavier traffic. My mother looked closely at the neon signs on the large pharmacies and American-style supermarkets. The vans hurried up and down the avenues and made sudden stops in the middle of the boulevards. My mother gasped each time we went by a large department store, shouting the names of places she had visited in years past.

The old hunchback got off at the iron market in Port-au-Prince. A few men with carts rushed to help her unload her charcoal bags from the roof.

She waved good-bye to us as the van pulled away.

"Find peace," she said, chewing the end of an unlit pipe.

"Find peace, you too." answered my mother.

Brigitte grabbed my blouse when she woke up. While I changed her diaper, my mother held my back and her head as though she was afraid that we would both crash if she let go. Brigitte slept peacefully through the rest of the trip.

"She's a good child," my mother said. "*C'est comme une poupée*. It's as if she's not here at all."

The airport lobby was crowded with peddlers, beggars, and travelers. We tried to keep up with the driver as he dashed towards a short line with our suitcases. My mother had no trouble at the reservation desk. Our American passports worked in our favor. She bribed the ticket seller twenty dollars to change us into seats next to one another.

I looked up at the murals on the high airport ceiling once more. The paintings of Haitian men and women selling beans, pulling carts, and looking very happy at their toil.

My mother's face looked purple on the flight. She left to go the bathroom several times. When she came back, she said nothing, just stared at the clouds out the window. The flight attendant gave her a pill, which seemed to calm her stomach.

"Is it the cancer again?" I asked.

"It's my discomfort with being in Haiti," she said. "I want to go back there only to be buried."

She picked at the white chicken they served us for lunch, while I gave Brigitte a bottle.

"You don't seem to eat much," she said.

"After I got married, I found out that I had something called bulimia," I said.

"What is that?"

"It's when you don't eat at all and then eat a whole lot— bingeing."

"How does that happen?" she said. "You are so tiny, so very petite. Why would you do that? I have never heard of a Haitian woman getting anything like that. Food, it was so rare when we were growing up. We could not waste it."

"You are blaming me for it," I said. "That is part of the problem."

"You have become very American," she said. "I am not blaming you. It is advice. I want to give you some advice. Eat. Food is good for you. It is a luxury. When I just came to this country I gained sixty pounds my first year. I couldn't believe all the different kinds of apples and ice cream. All the things that only the rich eat in Haiti, everyone could eat them here, dirt cheap."

"When I saw you for the first time, you were very thin."

"I had just gotten my breasts removed for the cancer. But before that, before the cancer. In the beginning, food was a struggle. To have so much to eat and not to eat it all. It took me a while to get used to the idea that the food was going to be there to stay. When I first came, I used to eat the way we ate at home. I ate for tomorrow and the next day and the day after that, in case I had nothing to eat for the next couple of days. I ate reserves. I would wake up and find the food still there and I would still eat ahead anyway."

"So it is not so abnormal that I have it," I said.

"You are different, but that's okay. I am different too. I want things to be good with us now."

My daughter was asleep by the time we landed in New York. My mother got our suitcases while I waited in the lobby.

"Will you spend the night at home before you go back to Providence?" she asked, struggling with our bags.

I told her I would.

"Don't you have someone you can call to pick us up?" I asked.

"The only person you have to count on is yourself," she said.

We took a cab back to Nostrand Avenue. I looked around the living room while she listened to the messages on her answering machine. There was still red everywhere, even the new sofa and love seat were a dark red velvet.

Most of her messages were from Marc. His voice sounded softer than I remembered it.

"*T'es retourné?*" Are you back?

"Call me as soon as you get back."

"*Je t'aime.*"

He even sounded excited on the "I love you." She moved closer to the machine, blocking my view of it, as though he was there in the flesh and she was standing with him and they were naked together.

I walked up the red carpeted stairs to my old room. Aside from the bed, the room was completely bare. She had removed all the jazz legend posters that Joseph had given me. On the far end of the wall was the sketch of her and me at Coney Island. The sketch emphasized the merry-go-round but shrunk us in comparison, except for our hands, which seemed like the largest parts of our bodies.

My old bed no longer creaked when I sat on it. My mother had fixed the noisy springs that had made it so much fun, so musical.

Her messages still echoed from downstairs. A final declaration of love from Marc and then one of her friends, asking where she was.

I opened my old closet. It too was empty. I went to the guest room, where she had a desk and a cot to do her reading and sewing. She had said that she would make it more homelike if ever my grandmother or Tante Atie decided to come for a visit.

The bed in her reading and sewing room squealed when I sat on it. My daughter liked the sound and laughed as we bounced up and down on it.

"Some things never change," my mother said, watching us from the doorway.

"I think we'll sleep here," I said.

"And your room?"

"The mattress there is too stiff."

"You can have my room," she said.

"Don't worry. It is only for one night."

"What about the baby?"

"She'll be okay with me."

"You're wondering what I've done with your things, aren't you?" she asked.

"I don't need those things anymore."

"I am sorry."

"Please don't be so sorry. I can always get others."

"I was passionately mad," she said.

"And you burnt them?"

"In a very frustrated moment, yes. I was having an anxiety attack and I took it out on those clothes."

"Better on the clothes than on yourself," I said.

"In spite of what I have done to you, you've really become an understanding woman," she said. "What do you want for dinner? We'll have no more of that bulimia. I'll cure it with some good food."

"It's not that simple."

"Then what are you supposed to do?"

"For now, I eat only when I'm hungry."

"Are you hungry now?" she asked.

"Not now."

"You didn't eat on the flight."

"Okay," I gave in. "I'll eat whatever you make."

"I need to go out after dinner," she said. "It's very important, otherwise I wouldn't lose this time with my daughter and granddaughter."

"We'll be fine."

I gave Brigitte a bath in the tub while my mother cooked spaghetti for dinner. The cooking smells of the house had changed.

We ate at the kitchen table, watching through the low windows as a little girl skipped rope under a hanging light in a neighbor's yard.

Brigitte tried to dig her pacifier into my plate. I cut off a strand of spaghetti and put it in her mouth.

"After you left home," she said, "the only thing I ate was

spaghetti. I would boil it and eat it quickly before I completely lost my appetite. Everything Haitian reminded me of you."

"It didn't have to be that way."

"I didn't realize you would call my bluff. I thought you would come back to me, humiliated."

She got up and cleared the table, leaving my full plate of spaghetti in front of me.

"I have to go now," she said.

"Are you still seeing Marc?" I asked.

"I want him to have dinner with you and your husband soon."

"So you're still seeing him."

"Very much *seeing* him."

"Are you going to marry him?"

"I have not even told *Manman* and Atie about him. At this point in my life, wouldn't it be senseless for me to marry?"

She grabbed her purse and started for the door.

"The sooner I go out, the sooner I can come back. I won't be long. If my phone rings, you can pick it up."

I dialed my home number from the living room phone. The answering machine picked up after the third ring. I heard my own voice, joyfully announcing that "You've reached the Woods residence. For Joseph, Sophie, or Brigitte, please leave a message."

I hung up quickly, not sure what to say to myself. I called again a few minutes later and left a message.

"Joseph, I'm back from Haiti. I'm in Brooklyn at my mother's. Please call me."

I left her number.

He called back a few minutes later.

"What's up?" he asked, as though we were just having a casual conversation.

"I'm okay and you?"

"Fine, except my wife left me."

"I am back. I'm at my mother's," I said.

"Is Brigitte okay?" he asked. "Can I speak to her?"

Brigitte grabbed the phone with both hands when I put it against her face.

"Is she okay?" he asked.

"She's fine."

"And you?"

"Good."

"Sophie, what were you thinking?"

"I'm sorry."

"Is this how we're going to handle all our problems? I was afraid something awful had happened to you. I call at all hours and you're never there. When I rush back to Providence all I get is a note. 'Sorry I needed to go somewhere and empty out my head.'"

"I wasn't away very long."

"What if your mother hadn't gone back for you? Wouldn't you have stayed longer?"

"I am back now, aren't I?"

"And what if you feel like leaving again?" he asked.

"Can we please talk about that later?"

"Are you coming home?"

"Yes."

"To stay?"

"What do you think?"

"I don't really know," he said. "What is it? What did I do, Sophie?"

"You know my problems."

"The therapy, that's helping you."

"I don't think it is."

"You'll have to start over, but you're okay."

"I don't feel okay."

"You're a beautiful woman. It's natural. You're desirable. Nothing is wrong with that."

"But we can't even *be together*."

"That's all right. I told you after the baby was born. As long as it takes, I will wait."

"But, what if I never get over it? What if I never get fixed?"

"You're not a machine. You can't go to a shop and get fixed. It will happen slowly. I've always told you this, haven't I? I will be there for you."

"Why didn't you answer the phone the first time?" I asked.

"I was practicing," he said. "Should I drive down and get you?"

"I told my mother I'd spend the night here with her. I'll rent a car and drive home tomorrow."

"All this traveling, isn't it rough on Brigitte?"

"She's got Caco blood. She's a strong one; she'll be fine."

"I want you to have the pediatrician check her out the minute you get home."

"I will."

"How's your mother?"

"She wants us all to have dinner with her male friend soon."

"You mean her boyfriend?"

"I suppose."

"I wouldn't have guessed that you went to Haiti. I wouldn't have known at all if it weren't for her. I was going to fly down to get you, but she wanted to find you herself."

"She didn't find me. I wasn't lost."

"You know what I mean."

"I know. My mother can be very overwhelming sometimes."

"She wanted to see you very badly. Did you work things out?"

"We talked," I said.

"Is she home? I'd like to thank her."

"You can thank her when you see her."

"And when will I see you?" he asked.

"Tomorrow."

"Are you sure?"

"Yes."

"There will be no pressure or anything," he said. "I promise you."

He wanted to hear Brigitte one more time. I tickled her feet and she laughed on cue.

"Does she speak Creole?" he asked.

"She didn't speak very much."

"She might have said Daddy and I missed it."

"She didn't."

"Is she walking on her own?"

"We've only been away a few days."

"It seems like ages. Does she still reach for people's food?"

"She does that."

"Can I come for you? I'll drive down there right now."

"It's better for me if I find my own way back. I am the one who left. I should come back myself."

I laid out a comforter in the guest room. I put the baby down on the guest bed, surrounded by four large pillows.

My mother walked in to check on us when she came home.

"Is everything all right?" she asked.

"Fine," I said. "How was your visit?"

"I went to see Marc." Her voice cracked. "I had something to tell him."

"Was it good? Was it bad?"

"Depends on how you look at it. Did you call your husband?"

"Yes."

"He will be happy to see you." She cradled the door as though she wasn't sure what to say next. "The baby, she's okay?"

"Fine," I said.

"Well, good night."

Chapter 29

∧∧∧∧∧∧∧∧∧

Breakfast was plentiful: all the things that made me feel most guilty when I ate them—bacon and eggs and extremely sweet café au lait.

"I thought you would be hungry," she said, "on the road to recovery. How can you resist all this food?"

"It's not as simple as that."

I had a piece of toast while my mother gave my daughter her formula. She looked like she hadn't slept much. The eggplant shade came back to her skin, as it always did before she applied her skin bleaching creams.

"You didn't look very happy when you came home last night," I said.

"Someone like me, you see me happy, you know I'm pretending," she said.

"Is something wrong?"

"Brace yourself. I know you are not going to believe what I have to tell you. Sophie, your mother is pregnant."

"Pregnant?" I stuttered.

"Marc and I, we have—"

"You sleep together?"

She nodded, looking ashamed.

"How far along are you?" I asked.

"A month or so."

"Are you going to marry him?"

"*Jesus Marie Joseph.* Am I going to do what?"

"Doesn't he want to marry you?"

"Of course he wants to marry me, but look at me. I am a fat woman trying to pass for thin. A dark woman trying to pass for light. And I have no breasts. I don't know when this cancer will come back. I am not an ideal mother."

Brigitte wrapped her arms around my mother's neck as my mother burped her.

"What are you going to do?" I asked.

"That's what I don't know."

"What does Marc want?"

"It's my decision. Supremely, it's mine. I am very scared. I don't know. The nightmares, they're coming back."

"In Dame Marie, it didn't seem like you slept at all."

"Whenever I'm there, I feel like I sleep with ghosts. The first night I was there, I woke up pounding at my stomach."

"What are you going to do about the baby?"

"I don't know."

"You can marry Marc and have the baby."

"And repeat my great miracle of being a super mother with you? Some things one should not repeat."

189

"Think of it as a second chance."

"I've had the second chance of my life by being spared death from this cancer. I can't ask too much."

"Do you love Marc?"

"I think I love him. Since you left, he stays with me at night and wakes me up when I have the nightmares."

"You still won't go for help?"

"I know I should get help, but I am afraid. I am afraid it will become even more real if I see a psychiatrist and he starts telling me to face it. God help me, what if they want to hypnotize me and take me back to that day? I'll kill myself. Marc, he saves my life every night, but I am afraid he gave me this baby that's going to take that life away."

"You can't say that."

"The nightmares. I thought they would fade with age, but no, it's like getting raped every night. I can't keep this baby."

"It must have been much harder then but you kept me."

"When I was pregnant with you, Manman made me drink all kinds of herbs, vervain, quinine, and verbena, baby poisons. I tried beating my stomach with wooden spoons. I tried to destroy you, but you wouldn't go away."

She reached over and handed Brigitte back to me.

"When I was carrying you, you were brave," she said. "You wanted to live. You wanted to taste salt, as my mother would say. You were going to kill me before I killed you."

"What are you going to do about this one?"

"She's a fighter too. She's already fighting me."

"Do you know that it's a girl?"

"I don't know. I never want to know. I think it's a girl because you ended up being a girl. I can't go through night

190

after night of the next nine months living these nightmares that same way again."

"Are you going to *take it out?*"

She crossed herself.

"*Jesus Marie Joseph.* Every time I even think of that, the nightmares get worse. It bites at the inside of my stomach like a leech. Last night after I talked to Marc about letting it go, I felt the skin getting tight on my belly and for a whole minute I couldn't breathe. I had to lie down and say I had changed my mind before I could breathe normally."

"Have you seen a doctor?"

"I know, these things, they sound crazy to me too, but maybe that's what it wants, to drive me crazy."

"You should talk to someone. Someone other than Marc, someone outside the whole situation."

"I am trying to keep one step ahead of a mental hospital. They would probably put me away, thinking that I might hurt both myself and this child."

"When you and Marc are *together*, do you have the nightmares then?"

"I pretend; it is like eating grapefruit. I was tired of being alone. If that's what I had to do to have someone wake me up at night, I would do it. But never in my life did I think I could get pregnant."

"You didn't use birth control?"

She laughed through her tears.

"I would have never imagined we could be having this conversation. Maybe if I spend more time with you, I will want this baby. I would want this child if the nightmares weren't so bad. I can't take them. One morning, I will wake up dead."

"Don't say that."

"You will leave today," she said.

"I can stay longer if you need me."

"Your husband, I know he will be anxious to see you."

"I can ask him to drive down and he will stay with us for a couple of days."

"Non non. I'll deal with this. Marc will come and stay here with me."

"Why don't you just marry him?"

"Because you don't marry someone to escape something that's inside your head. One night, I woke up and found myself choking Marc. This is before I knew I was pregnant. One day he'll get tired of it and leave me."

"What about the baby?"

"You've asked the same question a million ways; you have a camaraderie with this child. I'll have it. That's what you want to hear."

"At least this child will know its father."

"I will have it at the expense of my sanity. They will take it out of me one day and put me away the next."

She lent me her new car for the trip to Providence, a guarantee that I would come back to visit her. She tugged at Brigitte's hat and kissed her forehead as I strapped Brigitte into the back seat.

"You forgive me, don't you?" she asked.

I leaned over and kissed her stomach.

"It will be a beautiful baby," I said.

"Don't call it a baby."

I kept seeing her face as I drove into the New England

landscape. I knew the intensity of her nightmares. I had seen her curled up in a ball in the middle of the night, sweating and shaking as she hollered for the images of the past to leave her alone. Sometimes the fright woke her up, but most of the time, I had to shake her awake before she bit her finger off, ripped her nightgown, or threw herself out of a window.

After Joseph and I got married, all through the first year I had suicidal thoughts. Some nights I woke up in a cold sweat wondering if my mother's anxiety was somehow hereditary or if it was something that I had "caught" from living with her. Her nightmares had somehow become my own, so much so that I would wake up some mornings wondering if we hadn't both spent the night dreaming about the same thing: a man with no face, pounding a life into a helpless young girl.

I looked back at my daughter, who was sleeping peacefully. It was a good sign that at least she slept a lot, perhaps a bit more than other children. The fact that she could sleep meant that she had no nightmares, and maybe, would never become a frightened insomniac like my mother and me.

Chapter 30

∧∧∧∧∧∧∧∧∧

I pulled into the driveway of our house shortly after noon. Joseph nearly fell down the steps as he rushed towards the car. I screeched to a halt, a few inches shy of crashing into him.

He tapped on the back window, trying to get Brigitte's attention. She looked a bit disoriented when he raised her out of the seat.

"And the child's mother, does she get a hug?"

He pressed his lips down on mine.

"*Bienvenue*," he said, "Welcome back."

He ran up the steps with Brigitte, leaving me to carry my own bag.

The sun shining through the window colored our wooden floors the hue of Haitian dirt. Joseph threw Brigitte up in the air, both of them laughing as he caught her.

"Tell Daddy all about Haiti," he said.

Brigitte pursed her wet lips as though she wanted to.

"Are you glad to see Daddy?" He propped her up on the sofa.

"Are you glad to see her mommy?" I asked, sitting next to him.

"It's nice to see you, but I want to kill you."

His free hand traveled up and down my blouse.

"Did you miss me?" I asked.

"Sometimes."

The bedroom was messy. There were sheets piled on top of one another and pillows thrown randomly about. I held the sheets up to my face and sniffed them for another woman's scent. The mattress smelled like his socks.

"You see I need you to put some order in my life," he said.

"You need a maid," I said.

He twirled the duck mobile on the baby's crib, which we kept next to our bed.

"How was your trip?" he asked.

"My grandmother was preparing her funeral," I said. "It's a thing at home. Death is journey. My grandmother thinks she's at the end of hers."

"You called it home?" he said. "Haiti."

"What else would I call it?

"You have never called it that since we've been together. Home has always been your mother's house, that you could never go back to."

I searched through the pile of dishes in the kitchen sink, trying to find a clean glass for a drink of water. In the nursery were the large drums he sometimes used in performance.

"I was calling the ancestral spirits, asking them to make you come back to me," he said.

"Your prayers were answered."

I went to the living room and crashed on the sofa. It suddenly occurred to me that I was surrounded by my own life, my own four walls, my own husband and child. Here I was Sophie—*maîtresse de la maison*. Not a guest or visiting daughter, but the mother and sometimes, more painfully, the wife.

"We'll deal with this, won't we?" asked Joseph, pushing his tongue in my left ear. "I need to know that we can get through all this."

In the living room was a fuzzy picture of a very fat me lying naked with a newborn on my stomach. Joseph had been too excited to focus when we brought the baby home that first night. All I kept thinking was, Thank God it was a Caesarean section. The tearing from a natural birth would have totally destroyed me.

I reached over and tapped Brigitte's nose.

"I need to know. Did you leave on impulse or had you been planning to go for a long time?" he asked.

"We weren't connecting physically."

"Did you find an aphrodisiac?"

"I don't need an aphrodisiac. I need a little more understanding."

"I do understand. You are usually reluctant to start, but after a while you give in. You seem to enjoy it."

I called Brigitte's pediatrician to make an appointment. I gave Brigitte her bath, and laid her down while Joseph tapped a few keys on his saxophone.

I called my mother, but she did not pick up the phone. Her answering machine did not pick up either. I changed into a sweatsuit to go to bed. Joseph came to bed in a thick terry-cloth robe.

"If our skins touch," he said, "I won't be able to resist you."

We held each other while trying to make out the plot of an old black-and-white movie. It was about lovers, a young girl and her painting instructor.

At midnight, I called my mother.

She sounded anxious when she answered.

"What are you doing?" I asked.

"Marc is here with me," she said.

She told me she loved me and hung up the phone.

Joseph rocked me in his arms while we listened to the cooing sounds Brigitte made in her sleep.

"My mother is pregnant," I said.

"You will finally have a sibling, a kindred spirit."

It felt better when I thought of it that way.

"Brigitte will be older than her aunt," he said. "Isn't that nice?"

Our pediatrician, Karen, was happy to see Brigitte.

She was an middle-aged Indian woman who had sewn me up in the emergency room at the Providence hospital and had subsequently seen me through my pregnancy.

"Looks like you've lost weight," she said.

I held Brigitte's feet while she examined her.

I nearly dropped to my knees with gratitude when she told me that Brigitte was okay.

"We'll follow the regular schedule for checkups," she said, filling out her chart.

"Only a mountain can crush a Haitian woman," I said.

"In that case, your daughter has proven herself a real Haitian woman," Karen said.

"Tell me how it was," she asked as I dressed Brigitte after the physical. "You were going to the provinces, weren't you? There are warnings against all kinds of things in places like that."

"It is somewhat dry where I went. There are not a lot of swamps for malaria or any of those things you warned me about. I was careful about the baby's water. We always boiled it for a long time."

"She looks good so far, but keep an eye on her and call me if anything unusual happens. If you go to Haiti again any-time soon, leave your angel behind. I am not sure there's enough Haitian in her to survive another mountain."

I called Joseph from the hospital to tell him that everything was all right. When Brigitte and I came home, there was a large dinner waiting for us. Fried chicken, glazed potatoes, and broiled vegetables. Everything came frozen out of a box, but still managed to retain some flavor.

We decided to start giving Brigitte a few more adven-turous solids. I pureed some sweet potatoes and boiled some carrots and fed her small spoonfuls. I ate everything on my plate, forcing myself to resist the urge to purge my body.

After dinner, I called my mother.

"When are you going to come and have dinner with Marc and me?"

"We'll come as soon as we can," I said.

"How's the baby?"

"Good," I said, "How's yours?"

"Don't call it that," she said. "I haven't decided if I will follow through. It's fighting me though. More and more of a fighter every day."

"Is Marc there?"

"Yes, but he can sleep and I can't. I am watching television. I don't know. It's really hard. You know what happens now. I look at every man and I see him."

"Marc?"

"*Non non*," she whispered. "Him. *Le violeur*, the rapist. I see him everywhere."

"Have you told Marc?"

"He thinks my body is in shock from getting pregnant after all the cancer treatment."

"You should tell someone."

"You cannot report a ghost to the police."

Joseph's hands were creeping up my arm and going through the top of my nightgown.

"I tried to get rid of it," she said, "Today. But they wanted me to think about it for twenty-four hours. When I thought of taking it out, it got more horrifying. That's when I began seeing him. Over and over. That man who raped me."

"We'll come and visit you this weekend," I said.

"I want Joseph to meet Marc."

I felt his other hand creeping up my thighs, his hair smelling like aftershave as his face approached mine.

"*Manman*, I have to go," I said. "We'll visit with you on the weekend. Maybe Saturday."

"Saturday will be a wonderful day then," she said.

He reached over and pulled my body towards his. I closed my eyes and thought of the *Marassa*, the doubling. I was lying there on that bed and my clothes were being peeled off my body, but really I was somewhere else. Finally, as an adult, I had a chance to console my mother again. I was lying in bed with my mother. I was holding her and fighting off that man, keeping those images out of her head. I was telling her that it was all right. That it was not a demon in her stomach, that it was a child, like I was once a child in her body. I was telling her that I would never let anyone put her away in a mental hospital, that I would take care of her. I would visit her every night in my doubling and, from my place as a shadow on the wall, I would look after her and wake her up as soon as the nightmares started, just like I did when I was home.

I kept thinking of my mother, who now wanted to be my friend. Finally I had her approval. I was okay. I was safe. We were both safe. The past was gone. Even though she had forced it on me, of her sudden will, we were now even more than friends. We were twins, in spirit. *Marassas*.

"Can we visit my mother this weekend?" I asked Joseph.

"Whatever you want." He was panting.

"You were very good," he said.

"I kept my eyes closed so the tears wouldn't slip out."

I waited for him to fall asleep, then went to the kitchen. I ate every scrap of the dinner leftovers, then went to the bathroom, locked the door, and purged all the food out of my body.

Chapter 31

∧∧∧∧∧∧∧∧∧

There were three of us in my sexual phobia group. We gave it that name because that's what Rena—the therapist who introduced us—liked to call it.

Buki, an Ethiopian college student, had her clitoris cut and her labia sewn up when she was a girl. Davina, a middle-aged Chicana, had been raped by her grandfather for ten years.

We met at Davina's house. She was the only one of us with a place to herself. Buki lived in a college dorm and, of course, I lived with Joseph.

Davina had a whole room in her house set aside for our meetings. When we came in, we changed into long white dresses that Buki had sewn for us. We wrapped our hair in white scarves that I had bought. As we changed in the front room, I showed them the statue of Erzulie that my grandmother had given me. Davina told me to take it into the room myself, as I pondered what it meant in terms of my family.

The air in our room smelled like candles and incense. We sat on green heart-shaped pillows that Davina had made. The color green stood for life and growth.

We bowed our heads and recited a serenity prayer.

God grant us the courage to change those things we can, the serenity to accept the things we can't, and the wisdom to know the difference."

I laid the Erzulie next to our other keepsakes, the pine cones and seashells we collected on our solitary journeys.

"I am a beautiful woman with a strong body." Davina led the affirmations.

"We are beautiful women with strong bodies." We echoed her uncertain voice.

"Because of my distress, I am able to understand when others are in deep pain."

"Because of our distress, we are able to understand when others are in deep pain."

I heard my voice rise above the others.

"Since I have survived this, I can survive anything."

Buki read us a letter she was going to send to the dead grandmother who had cut off all her sexual organs and sewn her up, in a female rite of passage.

There were tears rolling down her face as she read the letter.

"Dear Taiwo. You sliced open my soul and then you told me I can't show it to anyone else. You took a great deal away from me. Because of you, I now carry with me an untouchable wound."

Sobbing, she handed me the piece of paper. I continued reading the letter for her.

"Because of you, I feel like a helpless cripple. I sometimes want to kill myself. All because of what you did to me, a child who could not say no, a child who could not defend herself. It would be easy to hate you, but I can't because you are part of me. You are me."

We each wrote the name of our abusers in a piece of paper, raised it over a candle, and watched as the flames consumed it. Buki blew up a green balloon. We went to Davina's backyard and watched as she released it in the dark. It was hard to see where the balloon went, but at least it had floated out of our hands.

I felt broken at the end of the meeting, but a little closer to being free. I didn't feel guilty about burning my mother's name anymore. I knew my hurt and hers were links in a long chain and if she hurt me, it was because she was hurt, too.

It was up to me to avoid my turn in the fire. It was up to me to make sure that my daughter never slept with ghosts, never lived with nightmares, and never had her name burnt in the flames.

When I came home from the meeting, I found Joseph sitting in the living room with Brigitte on his lap.

"Listen to this." He grabbed her and jumped up. "Say it again, pumpkin."

"Say what again?" I asked.

"She said Dada."

At his prodding, Brigitte said something that sounded like Dada.

"Say it again." We were both cheering.

Her eyes lit up as she watched us.

"Sweetie, say it again, please," I said, secretly rooting for "Mama."

She clapped her hands, keeping up with our excitement.

"Oh please, honey, say it again. Dada. Dada."

"Mama. Mama. *Manman.*"

She said Dada and laughed.

Joseph jumped up in the air and simulated a high five.

"She's saving Mama for when she can really talk," I said. "Dada is such a random sound."

"You're green with envy and you know it."

I went to the kitchen to make myself some tea.

"How was the meeting?" he asked.

"Good."

"Your mother called. She says she urgently needs to talk to you."

The baby was saying Dada over and over, trying to capture all his attention.

"Your therapist called too," he said. "She wanted to know if you'd be coming for your visit tomorrow. I said yes."

I let him play with the baby while I went in to call my mother.

"Marc is downstairs making me some eggs," she said.

"Are you all right?" I asked. "Joseph said it was urgent."

"It was an urgent feeling. I just wanted to hear your voice."

"Are you sure you're okay?"

"You think it's unhealthy, don't you? My sudden dependence on you."

"As long as you're all right."

"How is my granddaughter?"

"Fine. How about you? How is your situation?"

"I can't sleep. Are you coming this weekend?"

"On Saturday," I said.

"I am really happy we have this time again."

"Me too."

"I got a telegram from Manman today. She said everything is ready now for her funeral. She's glad about that."

"Did you tell her that you're pregnant?"

"I'll tell her when I'm further along. I don't want her to worry about me going crazy again."

"You sure you're feeling all right?"

"Better. Maybe this child, she's getting used to me. Manman tells me she's worried Atie will die from chagrin. Louise left a big hole in her. It's sad."

"She loved her."

"Atie will live. She always has."

I heard Marc's voice offering her some scrambled eggs.

"I'll wait for you on Saturday," she said.

"Bye, Mama."

"Bye, my star."

I sat up and wrote Tante Atie a letter. Now that she was reading, I wanted to send her something that only her eyes could see, something that she didn't have to have other people listen to. I imagined her standing there next to me, as we reminisced about the konbit potlucks, the lotteries we almost never won, and our dead relatives who we had such a kinship to, as though they were our restless spirits, shadows wandering in the darkness as our bodies slipped into bed.

Chapter 32

∧∧∧∧∧∧∧∧∧∧

My therapist was a gorgeous black woman who was an initiated Santeria priestess. She had done two years in the Peace Corps in the Dominican Republic, which showed in the brightly colored prints, noisy bangles, and open sandals she wore.

Her clinic was in a penthouse overlooking the Seekonk River. "You pulled a sudden disappearing act last week," she said as I looked over the collection of Brazilian paintings and ceremonial African masks on her walls.

She put out a cigarette while looking through my file. "Let's go for a stroll so you can tell me all about it."

We usually had our sessions in the woods by the river.

"So what is happening in your life?" she asked, waving a stick towards a stray dog behind us.

I told her about my sudden trip to Haiti, the trip that had caused me to miss my appointment the week before. I told her about my mother coming for me and my finding out that my grandmother, and her mother before her, had all been *tested*.

"I thought we were going to do some more work before you could actually try confrontational therapy," she said.

"I wasn't thinking about it as confrontational therapy. I just felt like going. And since Joseph was away I took advantage and went."

"I know a woman who went back to Brazil and took a jar full of dust from her mother's grave so she would always have her mother line with her. Did you have a chance to reclaim your mother line?"

"My mother line was always with me," I said. "No matter what happens. Blood made us one."

"You're telling me you never hated your mother."

"I felt a lot of pain."

"Did you hate her?" she asked.

"Maybe hate is not the right word."

"We all hate people at one time or another. If we can hate ourselves, why can't we hate other people?"

"I can't say I hated her."

"You don't want to say it. Why not?" she asked.

"Because it wouldn't be right, and maybe because it wouldn't be true."

"Maybe? You hesitate—"

"She wants to be good to me now," I said, "and I want to accept it."

"That's good."

"I want to forget the hidden things, the conflicts you always want me to deal with. I want to look at her as someone I am meeting again for the first time. An acquaintance who I am hoping will become a friend. I grew up believing that people could be in two places at once. Meeting for the first time again is not such a hard concept."

We watched a crew team paddling across the river.

"Did you ask your grandmother why they *test* their daughters?" she asked.

"To preserve their honor."

"Did you express your anger?"

"I tried, but it was very hard to be angry at my grandmother. After all she was only doing something that made her feel like a good mother. My mother too."

"And how was it, seeing your mother?"

"She is pregnant now."

"So she is in a relationship."

"It's the same man she was involved with when I was there."

"Are they married?"

"No."

"They sleep together?"

"Obviously."

"Did she sleep with him when you were home?" she asked.

"She would never have a man in the house when I was home. It would be a bad example."

"How does it make you feel knowing that she slept with someone? Don't you feel betrayed that after all these years, she does the very thing that she didn't want you to do?"

"I can't feel mad anymore."

A jogging couple bumped my shoulders as they raced by.

"Why aren't you mad anymore?" she asked.

"I feel sorry for her."

"Why?"

"The baby, it's roused up a lot of old emotions in my mother."

"What kinds of emotions?"

"Maybe emotions is not the word. It's brought back images of the rape."

"Like you did."

"Yes," I said. "Like I did."

"What about your father? Have you given him more thought?"

"I would rather not call him my father."

"We will have to address him soon. When we do address him, I'll have to ask you to confront your feelings about him in some way, give him a face."

"It's hard enough to deal with, without giving him a face."

"Your mother never gave him a face. That's why he's a shadow. That's why he can control her. I'm not surprised she's having nightmares. This pregnancy is bringing feelings to the surface that she had never completely dealt with. You will never be able to connect with your husband until you say good-bye to your father."

"I am seeing my mother this weekend," I said.

"You are establishing relations again."

"Joseph and I are going to visit her so we can get to know her friend."

"You mean her lover, the father of her child."

"Yes."

"Is it hard for you to imagine your mother sexually?"

"I've never really tried."

"Do it now."

"Do what?"

"Imagine her in the sexual act," she said.

I tried to imagine my mother, wincing and clenching her teeth as the large shadow of a man mounted her. She didn't like it. She even looked like she was crying, even though her lips were saying things that made him think otherwise.

"Do you imagine that it's the same for her as it is for you?"

"I imagine that she tries to be brave."

"Like you."

"Maybe."

"Do you think you'll ever stop thinking of what you and Joseph do as being brave?"

"I am his wife. There are certain things I need to do to keep him."

"The fear of abandonment. You always have that in the back of your mind, don't you?"

"I feel like my daughter is the only person in the world who won't leave me."

"Do you understand now why your mother was so adamantly against your being with a man, a much older man at that? It is only natural, dear heart. She also felt that you were the only person who would never leave her."

We stopped at a bench overlooking the river. Two swans were floating along trying to catch up with one another. The crew team was rowing towards the edge of the river.

"During your visit, did you go to the spot where your mother was raped?" Rena asked. "In the thick of the cane field. Did you go to the spot?"

"No, not really."

"What does that mean?"

"I ran past it."

"You and your mother should both go there again and see that you can walk away from it. Even if you can never face the man who is your father, there are things that you can say to the spot where it happened. I think you'll be free once you have your confrontation. There will be no more ghosts."

Chapter 33

∧∧·∧·∧·∧·∧·∧·∧∧

M y mother met us on the stoop outside the house. She was wearing a large tent dress with long puffy sleeves. She looked calmer, rested. Her skin was evened out with a powdered mahogany glow.

Joseph had driven in our station wagon, while I brought Brigitte in my mother's car.

"*Ca va byen?*" My mother kissed Joseph four times on the cheek. "I brought your wife and daughter back in one piece."

She took the baby from my arms and shoved Marc forward to introduce himself.

Marc was a bit fatter than I remembered. He was squeezed into a small gray jacket and a large pair of pants held up by suspenders.

Marc recited his full name as he shook Joseph's hand.

"Marc has a lot of the old ways," my mother said to Joseph.

The kitchen smelled like fried fish, boiled cabbage, and mayonnaise.

"What have you been up to?" my mother said, curling Brigitte up in her arms. Brigitte reached up to grab my mother's very short hair.

"She said Dada," Joseph announced proudly.

"Even when she grows up and gets a doctorate," Marc said, "it will not count as much."

Marc wrapped an apron around his waist and turned over the fish in the skillet.

My mother took Joseph on a tour of the house, the tour he had never gotten. He followed her obediently, beaming.

She moved us into the backyard where she had placed her picnic table near her hibiscus patch. She stood over Joseph's shoulder, to show him how to sprinkle chopped pickled peppers on his plantains.

"What kind of music do you do?" Marc asked Joseph as we sat down to eat.

"I try to do all kinds of music," Joseph said. "I think music should speak not only to the ear, but mostly to the soul."

"That's a very vague answer," my mother said.

"I think they want to know if you get paid," I said.

"We're not being as graceless as that," Marc said. "I was thinking more in terms of merengue, calypso, soka, samba?"

"Is there money in it?" asked my mother.

"I do okay," Joseph said. "I play with friends when they

2 1 3

need someone, but trust me, I have a little nest egg saved up."

My mother winked for only my eyes to see. She had prepared for this, was set to make Joseph love her. "I have something to tell you," she said to me. "I have made a decision."

Turning back to Joseph, my mother asked, "Is that how you bought your place in Providence?"

"Sure is," Joseph said.

"I really was asking more about your opinion of music," Marc insisted.

"We hear you," said my mother.

"He has much of the old ways," she whispered again in my ear.

Marc pretended not to hear.

"Where are your roots?" my mother asked Joseph as she fed plantain chunks to the baby.

"I was born in the South," he said. "Louisiana."

"They speak some kind of Creole there," she said.

"I know it," he said. "Sometimes I try to talk the little I know with my wife, your daughter."

"I feel like I could have been Southern," my mother said.

"We're all African," said Marc.

"Non non, me in particular," said my mother. "I feel like I could have been Southern African-American. When I just came to this country, I got it into my head that I needed some religion. I used to go to this old Southern church in Harlem where all they sang was Negro spirituals. Do you know what Negro spirituals are?" she said turning to Marc.

Marc shrugged.

"I try to get him to church," my mother said, "just to listen to them, but he won't go. You tell him, Joseph. Tell this old Haitian, with his old ways, about a Negro spiritual."

"They're like prayers," Joseph said, "hymns that the slaves used to sing. Some were happy, some sad, but most had to do with freedom, going to another world. Sometimes that other world meant home, Africa. Other times, it meant Heaven, like it says in the Bible. More often it meant freedom."

Joseph began to hum a spiritual.

Oh Mary, don't you weep!

"That's a Negro spiritual," said my mother.

"It sounds like *vaudou* song," said Marc. "He just described a *vaudou* song. *Erzulie, don't you weep,*" he sang playfully.

"I told you I could have been Southern." My mother laughed.

"Do you have a favorite Negro spiritual?" Joseph asked my mother.

"I sure do."

"Give us a rendition," urged Marc.

"You'll regret asking," said my mother.

"All of you will help me if I stumble." She rocked Brigitte's body to the solemn lift of her voice.

> Sometimes I feel like a motherless child.
> Sometimes I feel like a motherless child.
> Sometimes I feel like a motherless child.
> A long ways from home.

We all clapped when she was done. Brigitte, too.

"I want that sung at my funeral," my mother said. "My

mother's got me thinking this way; you've got to plan for everything."

The day ended too soon for my mother. We never got a moment alone for her to tell me what she had decided. That night as we said good-bye, she wrapped her arms around my body and would not let go.

"She will come back," Marc said, separating us.

"Us Caco women," she said, "when we're happy, we're very happy, but when we're sad, the sadness is deep."

On the ride back to Providence, Joseph kept singing my mother's spiritual, adding some bebop to the melody, as though to reverse the sad tone.

"Your mother's good folk," he said. "I always understood why she didn't like me. She didn't want to give up a gem like you."

My mother had left two messages on our machine by the time we got home.

"We had a nice day, *pa vrè?*" she said when I called back. "Did Joseph enjoy himself? The two of you, you go very well together. Marc thought he was old for you, but he liked meeting him anyway."

She stopped to catch her breath.

"Are you really okay?" I asked.

"It was wonderful to see you."

"The nightmares, have they stopped?"

"I didn't tell you what I had decided. I am going to get it out of me."

"When did you decide?"

"Last night when I heard it speak to me."

"Are you sure?"

"Yes. I am sure, it spoke to me. It has a man's voice, so now I know it's not a girl. I am going to get it out of me. I am going to get it out of me, as the stars are my witness."

"Don't do anything rash."

"Everywhere I go, I hear it. I hear him saying things to me. You *tintin, malpròp*. He calls me a filthy whore. I never want to see this child's face. Your child looks like *Manman*. This child, I will never look into its face."

"But it's Marc's child."

"What if there is something left in me and when the child comes out it has that other face?"

"You mean what if it looks like me?"

"No, that is not what I mean."

"Marc has no children; he must want some."

"If he wants some badly enough, he can have some."

I heard Marc asking who she was talking to.

"I'll call you tomorrow," she said before hanging up. "Pray to the Virgin Mother for me."

Chapter 34

∧∧∧∧∧∧∧∧∧∧∧

I had a late afternoon session on the bare floor of Rena's office. Through her smoked French doors, the river looked a breathless blue.

"How was the visit with your mother?" she asked.

"I am very worried about her state of mind," I said. "It was like two people. Someone who was trying to hold things together and someone who was falling apart."

"You feel she was only pretending to be happy."

"Deep inside, yes."

"Why?"

"That's always how she's survived. She feels that she has to stay one step ahead of a mental institution so she has to hold it together at least on the surface."

"What has she decided to do with the baby?"

"She is probably taking it out as we speak."

"What do you mean she's *taking it out?*"

"*Losing* it. *Dropping* it. I can't say it."

"An abortion?"

"Yes."

"Why?"

"She says she hears the baby saying things to her. He says hurtful things, this baby."

"Your mother hears a voice?"

"Yes."

"Has she always heard voices?"

"When I lived with her, it was just the nightmares, her reliving the experience over and over again."

"And now she hears these voices?"

"Yes."

"If she's afraid of therapy, perhaps your mother should have an exorcism."

"An exorcism?"

"I am not joking. She should have a release ritual. The kind of things you do with the sexual phobia group. You can help."

"She is afraid to deal with anything that would make this more real."

"It has to become frighteningly real before it can fade."

"It's always been real to her," I said. "Twenty-five years of being raped every night. Could you live with that? This child, it makes the feelings stronger. It takes her back to a time when she was carrying me. Even the time when she was living with me. That's why she is trying to get the child out of her body."

"I think she needs an exorcism. Has she told her lover that she wants to abort?"

"I wish you wouldn't call him that."

"Why not?"

"It sounds—" I hesitated.

"Sexual?"

"Yes."

"Too sexual to be linked with your mother? I think you have a Madonna image of your mother. Part of you feels that this child is a testimonial of her true sexuality. It's a child she conceived willingly. Maybe even she is not able to face that."

"I just want her to be okay," I said.

"Does her lover know that she doesn't want the baby?"

"The way my mother acts, he probably think it's the best thing that's ever happened to her. I don't think she's ever really explained to him about how I was born."

"Do you think he would want her to have the baby?"

"Not if he knew what it was doing to her. I don't think so."

"And you think she's aborting right now?"

"Before I came here, I called her and she wasn't there. I called her at work and she wasn't there."

"So she's going to do this on her own. Without her lover."

"I think she'll lose her mind if she doesn't."

"I really think you should convince her to seek help."

"I can't convince her," I said. "She's always thought that she was crazy already, that she had just fooled everybody."

"It's very dangerous for her to go on like she is."

"I know."

I drove past Davina's house. She was at work, but I had my own key to our room. I went in and sat in the dark and drank some verbena tea by candlelight. The flame's shadows swayed across Erzulie's face in a way that made it seem as though she was crying.

On the way out, I saw Buki's balloon. It was in a tree, trapped between two high branches. It had deflated into a little ball the size of a green apple.

We thought it had floated into the clouds, even hoped that it had traveled to Africa, but there it was slowly dying in a tree right above my head.

Chapter 35

∧∧∧∧∧∧∧∧∧∧∧

Joseph was on the couch, rocking the baby, when I came home. She was sleeping in his arms, with her index and middle fingers in her mouth. Joseph took her to our room and put her down without saying a word. He came back and pulled me down on the sofa. He picked up the answering machine and played me a message from Marc.

"Sophie, *je t'en prie*, call me. It's about your mother."

Marc's voice was quivering, yet cold. It seemed as though he was purposely forcing himself to be casual.

I grabbed Joseph's collar, almost choking him.

"Let's not jump to any wild conclusions," he said.

"I am wondering why she is not calling me herself," I said.

"Maybe she's had a complication with the pregnancy."

"She was going to have an abortion today."

"Keep calm and dial."

The phone rang endlessly. Finally her answering machine picked up. "*S'il vous plait, laissez-moi un message*. Please leave me a message." Impeccable French and English, both painfully mastered, so that her voice would never betray the fact that she grew up without a father, that her mother was merely a peasant, that she was from *the hills*.

We sat by the phone all night, alternating between dialing and waiting.

Finally at six in the morning, Marc called.

His voice was laden with pain.

"Sophie. *Je t'en prie*. I am sorry."

He was sobbing.

"What is it?" I asked.

"*Calme-toi*. Listen to me."

"Listen to what?"

"I am sorry," he said.

"Put my mother on the phone. What did you do?"

"It's not me."

"Please, Marc. Put my mother on the phone. Where is she? Is she in the hospital?"

He was sobbing. Joseph pressed his face against mine. He was trying to listen.

"Is my mother in the hospital?"

"*Non*. She is rather in the morgue."

I admired the elegance in the way he said it. Now he would have to say it to my grandmother, who had lost her daughter, and to my Tante Atie, who had lost her only sister.

"Am I hearing you right?" I asked.

"She is gone."

Joseph pressed harder against me.

"What happened?" I was shouting at Marc.

223

"I woke up in the middle of the night. Sometimes, I wake up and she's not there, so I was not worried. Two hours passed and I woke up again, I went to the bathroom and she was lying there."

"Lying there? Lying where? Talk faster, will you?"

"In blood. She was lying there in blood."

"Did she slip and fall?"

"It was very hard to see."

"What was very hard to see?"

"She had a mountain of sheets on the floor. She had prepared this."

"What?"

"She stabbed her stomach with an old rusty knife. I counted, and they counted again in the hospital. Seventeen times."

"Are you sure?"

"It was seventeen times."

"How could you sleep?" I shouted.

"She was still breathing when I found her," he said. "She even said something in the ambulance. She died there in the ambulance."

"What did she say in the ambulance?"

"*Mwin pa kapab enkò*. She could not carry the baby. She said that to the ambulance people."

"How could you sleep?" I was screaming at him.

"I did the best I could," he said. "I tried to save her. Don't you know how I wanted this child?"

"Why did you give her a child? Didn't you know about the nightmares?" I asked.

"You knew better about the nightmares," he said, "but where were you?"

I crashed into Joseph's arms when I hung up the phone.

It was as if the world started whirling after that, as though I had no control over anything. Everything raced by like a speeding train and I, breathlessly, sprang after it, trying to keep up.

I grabbed my suitcase from the closet and threw a few things inside.

"I am going with you," Joseph said.

"What about Brigitte? Who will look after her? I can't take her into this."

"Let's sit down and think of some way."

I didn't have time to sit and think.

"You stay. I go. It's that simple."

He didn't insist anymore. He helped me pack my bag. We woke up the baby and he drove me to the bus station.

We held each other until the bus was about to pull out.

I gave Brigitte a kiss on the forehead.

"Mommy will bring you a treat from the market."

She began to cry as I boarded the bus. Joseph took her away quickly, not looking back.

Marc was waiting in the house in Brooklyn when I got there. Somehow I expected there to be detectives, and flashing cameras, but this was New York after all. People killed themselves every day. Besides, he was a lawyer. He knew people in power. He simply had to tell them that my mother was crazy.

There was a trail of dried blood, down from the stairs to the living room and out to the street where they must have loaded her into the ambulance. The bathroom floor was spotless, however, except for the pile of bloody sheets stuffed in trash bags in the corner.

"Sophie, will you sit down?" Marc said, following me as I raced in and out of every room in the house. "I need to tell you how things will proceed."

I rushed into my mother's room. It was spotless and her bed was properly made. In her closet, everything was in some shade of red, her favorite color since she'd left Haiti.

"I was cleared beyond any doubt in your mother's *accident*. I have used what influence I have to make this very expeditious for all of us. I have contacted a funeral home. They will get her from the morgue and they will ship her to a funeral home in Dame Marie."

If I died mute, I would never speak to him again. I would never open my mouth and address a word to him.

"We can see her in the funeral home," he said. "They will ship her tomorrow night. That's the earliest possible. They have a service. They notify the family. I have already had your family notified."

How dare he? How could he? To send news that could kill my grandmother, by telegram.

"You can sleep at my house until the flight tomorrow night."

I had no intention of going to his house. I was going to spend the night right there, in my mother's house.

He did not leave me. He stayed in the living room and ate Chinese food while I crouched in the fetal position in the large bed in my mother's room.

Joseph let me listen to Brigitte's giggles when I called home. I heard a voice say Mama, but I knew it was his. She was still saying Dada, even though I knew he had tried to coach her.

"One day we'll all take a trip together," he said.

"This trip I must make alone."

"We are waiting for you," he said, "we love you very much. Don't stay there too long."

I lay in my mother's bed all night fighting evil thoughts: It is your fault that she killed herself in the first place. Your face took her back again. You should have stayed with her. If you were here, she would not have gotten pregnant.

When I woke up the next day, Marc was asleep on the sofa.

"Would you pick something for your mother to be buried in?" he asked.

He spoke to me the way older men addressed orphan children, with pity in his voice. If we had been in Haiti, he might have given me a penny to ease my pain.

I picked out the most crimson of all my mother's clothes, a bright red, two-piece suit that she was too afraid to wear to the Pentecostal services.

It was too loud a color for a burial. I knew it. She would look like a Jezebel, hot-blooded Erzulie who feared no men, but rather made them her slaves, raped them, and killed them. She was the only woman with that power. It was too bright a red for burial. If we had an open coffin at the funeral home, people would talk. It was too loud a color for burial, but I chose it. There would be no ostentation, no viewing, neither pomp nor circumstance. It would be simple like she had wanted, a simple prayer at the grave site and some words of remembrance.

"Saint Peter won't allow your mother into Heaven in that," he said.

"She is going to Guinea," I said, "or she is going to be a star. She's going to be a butterfly or a lark in a tree. She's going to be free."

He looked at me as though he thought me as insane as my mother.

At my mother's dressing, in the Nostrand Avenue funeral home, her face was a permanent blue. Her eyelids were stretched over her eyes as though they had been sewn shut.

I called Joseph one last time before we got on the plane. He put the baby on the phone to wish me *Bon Voyage*. This time she said *Manman*. When I said good-bye, she began to cry.

"She feels your absence," Joseph said.

"Does she sleep?" I asked.

"Less now," he said.

My mother was the heavy luggage that went under the plane. I did not sit next to Marc on the plane. There were enough seats so that I did not have to. There were not many people going to Haiti, only those who were in the same circumstances as we were, going to weddings or funerals.

At the airport in Port-au-Prince, he spun his head around to look at everything. It had been years since he had left. He was observing, watching for changes: In the way the customs people said *Merci* and *au revoir* when you bribed them not to search your bags. The way the beggars clanked the pennies in their tin cans. The way the van drivers nearly killed one another on the airport sidewalk to reach you. The way young girls dashed forward and offered their bodies.

He had been told by the funeral home that my mother's body would follow us to the Cathedral Chapel in Dame Marie. A funeral home driver would pick her up. As soon as she got there, we could claim her and bury her, that same day, if that's what we wanted. The chauffeur arrived promptly and gave us a ride, in the hearse, to Dame Marie.

I felt my body stiffen as we walked through the maché in Dame Marie. Marc had his eyes wide open, watching. He looked frightened of the Macoutes, one of whom was sitting in Louise's stand selling her last colas.

People greeted me with waves and smiles on the way to my grandmother's house. It was as though I had lived there all my life.

Marc was straining to take in the sights. We walked silently. Louise's shack looked hollow and empty when we went by. In the cane fields, the men were singing about a mermaid who married a fisherman and became human.

My grandmother was sitting on the porch with her eyes on the road. I wondered how long she had been sitting there. For hours, through the night, since she had heard? We ran to each other. I told her everything. What I knew from him, where I blamed myself, and where he had blamed me.

She knew, she said, she knew even before she was told. When you let your salt lay in the sun, you are always looking out for rain. She even knew that my mother was pregnant. Remember, all of us have the gift of the unseen. Tante Atie was sitting on the steps with a black scarf around her head.

She was clinging to the porch rail, now with two souls to grieve for.

Marc introduced himself to my grandmother, reciting his whole name.

"Dreams move the wind," said my grandmother. "I knew, but she never spoke of you."

We decided to have the funeral the next morning, just among ourselves. That night we made a large pot of tea, which we shared with only Eliab and the other wandering boys. We did not call it a wake, but we played cards and drank ginger tea, and strung my wedding ring along a thread while singing a festive wake song: Ring sways to Mother. Ring stays with Mother. Pass it. Pass it along. Pass me. Pass me along.

Listening to the song, I realized that it was neither my mother nor my Tante Atie who had given all the mother-and-daughter motifs to all the stories they told and all the songs they sang. It was something that was essentially Haitian. Somehow, early on, our song makers and tale weavers had decided that we were all daughters of this land.

Marc slept in Tante Atie's room while Tante Atie slept in my grandmother's bed with her. They allowed me the courtesy of having my mother's bed all to myself.

The next day, we went together to claim my mother's body. My grandmother was wearing a crisp new black dress. She would surely wear black to her grave now. Tante Atie was wearing a purple frock. I wore a plain white dress, with a purple ribbon for my daughter. We sat on the plush velvet in the funeral chapel, waiting for them to bring her out. Tante Atie was numb and silent. My grandmother was watching for the black priest, the one they call Lavalas, to come through the door. The priest was the last missing pebble in the stream. Then we could take my mother to the hills.

Marc got up and walked around, impatiently waiting for them to wheel out her coffin. The velvet curtains parted and a tall mulatto man theatrically pushed the coffin forward.

Marc raised the olive green steel lid and felt the gold satin lining. My mother was lying there with a very calm look on her face. I reached over to brush off some of the melting rouge, leaving just enough to accentuate her dress.

She didn't feel as cold as I expected. She looked as though she was dressed for a fancy affair and we were all keeping her from going on her way. Marc was weeping into his handkerchief. He reached into his vest pocket and pulled out a small Bible. He reached in and folded her hands over it. My grandmother dropped in a few threadless needles and Tante Atie, one copper penny.

My grandmother did not look directly at my mother's face, but at the red gloves on her hands and the matching shoes on her feet. My grandmother looked as though she was going to fall down, in shock.

We pulled her away and led her back to her seat. The priest came in and sprinkled holy water on my mother's forehead. He was short and thin, a tiny man with bulging eyes. He leaned forward and kissed my grandmother's hands. He crossed himself and held my grandmother's shoulder. Tante Atie fell on the ground; her body convulsing.

Marc grabbed her and held her up. Her body slowly stilled but the tears never stopped flowing down her face.

"Let us take her home," said my grandmother.

They took her coffin up the hill in a cart. My grandmother walked in front with the driver and Tante Atie and I walked behind with the priest. As we went through the market, a crowd of curious observers gathered behind us.

We soon collected a small procession, people who recognized my grandmother and wanted to share her grief. The vendors ran and dropped their baskets at friends' houses, washed their feet and put on their clean clothes to follow my mother. School children trailed us in a long line. And in the cane fields, the men went home for their shirts and then joined in.

The ground was ready for my mother. Somehow the hole seemed endless, like a bottomless pit. The priest started off with a funeral song and the whole crowd sang the refrain.

> Good-bye, brother. Good-bye, sister.
> Pray to God for us.
> On earth we see you nevermore
> In heaven we unite.

People with gourd rattles and talking drums joined in. Others chimed in with cow horns and conch shells. My grandmother looked down at the grave, her eyes avoiding the coffin. Some of the old vendors held Tante Atie, keeping her body still.

My grandmother threw the first handful of dirt on the coffin as it was lowered into the ground. Then Tante Atie, and then me. I threw another handful for my daughter who was not there, but was part of this circle of women from whose gravestones our names had been chosen.

From the top of the hill, I saw our house, between the hills and the cane field.

I couldn't bear to see them shoveling dirt over my mother. I turned around and ran down the hill, ahead of the others. I felt my dress tearing as I ran faster and faster down the hill.

There were only a few men working in the cane fields. I ran through the field, attacking the cane. I took off my shoes and began to beat a cane stalk. I pounded it until it began to lean over. I pushed over the cane stalk. It snapped back, striking my shoulder. I pulled at it, yanking it from the ground. My palm was bleeding.

The cane cutters stared at me as though I was possessed. The funeral crowd was now standing between the stalks, watching me beat and pound the cane. My grandmother held back the priest as he tried to come for me.

From where she was standing, my grandmother shouted like the women from the market place, "Ou libéré?" Are you free?

Tante Atie echoed her cry, her voice quivering with her sobs.

"Ou libéré!"

There is always a place where women live near trees that, blowing in the wind, sound like music. These women tell stories to their children both to frighten and delight them. These women, they are fluttering lanterns on the hills, the

233

fireflies in the night, the faces that loom over you and recreate the same unspeakable acts that they themselves lived through. There is always a place where nightmares are passed on through generations like heirlooms. Where women like cardinal birds return to look at their own faces in stagnant bodies of water.

I come from a place where breath, eyes, and memory are one, a place from which you carry your past like the hair on your head. Where women return to their children as butterflies or as tears in the eyes of the statues that their daughters pray to. My mother was as brave as stars at dawn. She too was from this place. My mother was like that woman who could never bleed and then could never stop bleeding, the one who gave in to her pain, to live as a butterfly. Yes, my mother was like me.

From the thick of the cane fields, I tried my best to tell her, but the words would not roll off my tongue. My grandmother walked over and put her hand on my shoulder.

"Listen. Listen before it passes. *Paròl gin pié zèl*. The words can give wings to your feet. There is so much to say, but time has failed you," she said. "There is a place where women are buried in clothes the color of flames, where we drop coffee on the ground for those who went ahead, where the daughter is never fully a woman until her mother has passed on before her. There is always a place where, if you listen closely in the night, you will hear your mother telling a story and at the end of the tale, she will ask you this question: '*Ou libéré?*' Are you free, my daughter?"

My grandmother quickly pressed her fingers over my lips.

"Now," she said, "you will know how to answer."